PIRATE
DOG

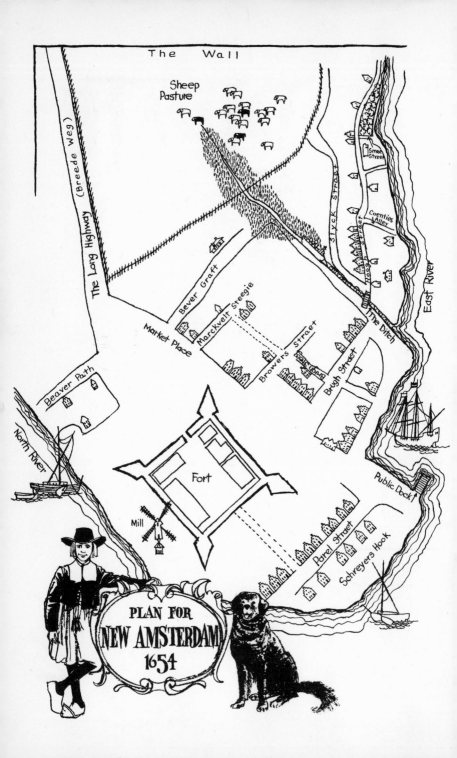

The Wall

Sheep Pasture

The Long Highway (Breede Weg)

Smee Street

Slyck Street

Coenties Alley

East River

Bever Graft

Marckvelt steegie

Market Place

Browers Straet

Brugh Street

The Ditch

Beaver Path

North River

Fort

Mill

Public Dock

Parel Straet

Schreyers Hook

PLAN FOR
NEW AMSTERDAM
1654

PIRATE DOG

BY Cathrine S. Cleven

Author of *The Secret of the King's Field*

Illustrated by

LESLIE GOLDSTEIN

THE **BOBBS-MERRILL** COMPANY, INC.
A SUBSIDIARY OF HOWARD W. SAMS & CO., INC.
Publishers • INDIANAPOLIS • NEW YORK

jC5991p

To my husband Edmund

Contents

CHAPTER ONE

Who Am I?

A DOG WHIMPERED. The boy opened his eyes slowly and saw it still was light. The storm had passed, and he was lying beside a black rock on a patch of sand.

He put his hand to his aching head. There was blood on his fingers when he brought them back. Something must have struck him. But what? He could remember nothing.

"How did I come to this place?" he whispered. "Where am I?"

He felt a warm body pressing close against his wet clothes. He rolled his eyes slightly. A large black dog lay next to him and watched him with bright brown eyes.

"You!" the boy croaked. "Where did you come from?"

He tried to sit up but could not. He put out his hand and ran it over the dog's slightly oily fur. The square muzzle felt a little damp. The dog's long tail beat a friendly thump on the hard sand.

The boy shivered. He seemed to have a foggy memory of a bad storm at sea. "Did you save me?" he said to the dog.

But the animal only cocked his head as if he did not understand the boy's Dutch speech. Suddenly he raised his eyes past the boy. The hair on his back stood straight up, and a growl rumbled in his deep chest. The black dog jumped to his feet.

The next moment the boy saw a wild-looking man with cinnamon brown skin standing near him. The wild man carried a fish net in his hands.

The boy gulped as he stared into the glittering eyes and saw the feather in the black hair, and the bare chest. He was aware of the strong smell of rancid animal grease on the man's body. Then he saw the red man draw back fearfully as the big dog gave another warning growl.

The boy put out his hand to hold back the dog, who was ready to spring. "Wait," he said feebly. He looked at the man. "Who are you?"

He had seen pictures of the "Wilden," the name the Dutch settlers had given the Indians of the New

10

World. Was this the New World? he wondered.

The man spoke a few strange words, pointing to the boy then toward the thin woods behind them. He turned and disappeared.

"He's gone to get his scalping tools," the boy said to the dog and tried to laugh at his own joke.

He shivered again. How could he get help? And would the savage come back and take him prisoner?

He tried to get up again and fell back with a groan. If only he could crawl away and hide before the red man returned. How helpless he felt lying there too weak to move.

Now the dog began to run back and forth along the rocks and water's edge. He came back to the boy, then turned his nose toward the water and sniffed.

Suddenly he gave a short bark. He waded out into the water past the large rock.

"Ho there!" A Dutch voice came over the water. A moment later the boy heard the swish of an oar and next a boat being dragged up on shore.

His head hurt too much to turn it again to see who it was. But he heard footsteps clumping over the hard sand. At least he's not a savage, the boy thought.

"Help me, please," he called out. "Over here. I'm hurt."

A man in rough fisherman's clothes leaned over

11

him. The boy looked up into a weathered face covered by a rusty beard streaked with white. The fisherman's eyes were the pale blue of a spring sky and hard as hailstones. He wore a red knit stocking cap.

"A shipwrecked lad, by a whale's flippers!" he growled. "Or are you a runaway? Where you from . . . who are you?"

Who am I? The boy tried to think, but his head was still dizzy. "I'm from a ship, I think . . . I . . . I . . . can't recall its name. There was a storm and my head . . . where am I, in the New World?"

"Well I'll be . . . of course! This is Long Island in the New Netherlands," the man said in surprise.

So it was the New World! Then the boy thought of the wild man. "A savage was here. He went away a little while ago. Maybe he'll be back soon."

"Ach! We must hurry." The fisherman caught the boy under his arms and half dragged, half carried him to the boat. "Maybe a Canarse, or a Matinnecock," he muttered. "Either one might take you prisoner if they think you'll bring a ransom. They are not too friendly with us Dutch or with the English settlements here on Long Island."

For some reason the dog had not growled at the newcomer. When the man laid the boy in the bottom of his boat, the dog jumped in, too, and sat in the bow.

"Saw some floating wreckage after the storm. Thought I'd look around to see what I could find," the fisherman said after he climbed into his boat. "You're all I found."

"My thanks to you," the boy said from his heart.

Nothing more was said as the fisherman's strong arms pulled away in steady strokes. After what seemed a long while he said, "Gave them the slip. Now what am I going to do with you, boy?"

But the boy drifted off to sleep under a piece of old canvas without answering him. He was safe from capture and safe from the sea. That was enough for the moment. He would think about who he was later.

When the boy awoke at dawn he found himself in a one-room log cabin. He was lying on a sleeping bunk built in one corner. He touched the swollen cut in his head. The man who called himself Kryn had bound his wound with a dressing of some sort and a rag. The bump throbbed painfully, but he felt stronger after his sleep.

The fisherman was pouring soup from the fireplace kettle into wood bowls. He turned, bowl in hand, to meet the boy's eyes.

"Ach, you're awake. Good." Kryn pulled over a stool to the bunk and sat down. Without more ado, Kryn began pushing a wooden spoonful of oyster stew into the boy's mouth. "Eat, boy," he ordered.

After the first taste, the boy knew he was very hungry. He ate greedily until every drop was gone. Then he lay back on the straw with a sigh. "Thank you, Mynheer Kryn."

"I'm just plain Kryn, the oysterman, I'm no 'My sir.' And don't think I like doing this!" the fisherman said.

He sat down at his rough table and began to eat his stew. "Busy man!" he said between huge mouthfuls. "Load of fine oysters ready and waiting for my trader's sloop from Massachusetts Bay colony. Why doesn't he come?" He glared at the boy as if it were his fault. "He has a sloop stop here on its way to the English villages here on Long Island. You see, we have the world's finest oysters in this bay."

The boy didn't know what to say. Then he heard Kryn ask again the question he'd been dreading. "Who are you, boy?"

"My name is . . . is . . . " he began and then his lips shook. He could not remember his name. He did not know where he came from, or how he got

14

on a ship . . . at least he thought he'd been on a ship.

"I don't know, Kryn. I can't remember anything. My mind is fuzzy." He sat up and the room swam about him.

"This is April, 1654. Do you remember that? You wear good Dutch clothes. Are you from the Netherlands back home, or from New Amsterdam or Breucklen here?" Kryn frowned at the boy.

"No, from . . . ah . . . I can guess I was on this ship and it sank in the storm. That's all I know." The boy put his hand to his head. "Maybe when my head stops hurting I can think better. But I'm sure the dog rescued me." He looked up at Kryn. "Is he yours?"

"That black dog outside? Ach, no! He is stupid. He won't go away." Kryn sounded disgusted.

There came a scratching at the door and a whimper.

"Oh, he's still here, then. That's good!" The boy gave a little laugh although it hurt his head. "I think he's a smart dog to rescue me from that terrible water. He saved my life. Whose dog is he?"

"I don't know. I live alone here, and I haven't seen him at any of the Dutch or English villages on the island. Wasn't he from your ship? Wasn't anyone else saved?"

The boy flung out his hand helplessly. "I just can't remember. There was no one else on shore. May the dog come in? He's cold."

"No!" Kryn removed the bandage and herb dressing to inspect the boy's wound. "The herbs have stopped the bleeding. Long Mary, that old witch, knows her medicine well. A surgeon ought to look at it." He tied the rag around the boy's yellow hair again.

"I'm feeling better," the boy told him.

"Good. Your clothes are dry. Put them on." As the boy did so, Kryn continued, "Ach, I can't wait here for that sloop until my fine oysters spoil. I'm going to take them to market at New Amsterdam. It's on Manhattes Island, a brisk sail down the Sound. You might find help there at the Town Hall. *I'll* not keep you."

"I'm ready to go with you to New Amsterdam," the boy said. What else could he do? He set his teeth, got up, then swayed.

Kryn's big arm went around him. "Stay your oars! You need help to get out to my boat. It's loaded and ready to go."

Outside the little hut the morning sun slanted its rays over wide Oyster Bay. The sky was clear of storm clouds. They were on a hook of land jutting out into the entrance to the bay. Looking back into the bay, the boy could see several boats and a few log houses.

"English over there." Kryn sniffed in disgust. "Always trying to push into our Dutch land! We were here first. They've been high and mighty since the sea war between our United Netherlands Republic and England started two years ago."

"A sea war! Have you had real battles here?" the boy asked, his eyes wide.

"No. So far it's been a war between our mother countries, and we've been at peace in the New World." Kryn scowled. "Now we hear rumors that New England plans to raise an army against us. So our English settlers forget the oaths of allegiance they made to New Netherlands when they came here to live. They want to turn all of Long Island over to the New England plantations." He waved his arm to the north.

"But why do the English have villages on our Long Island at all?" The boy asked it because he felt Kryn wanted him to do so.

"That's what all us good folk wonder, since Hendrik Hudson discovered this part of the New World for us Dutch," Kryn declared.

Hendrik Hudson! The boy felt that name should

mean something to him, but what, he couldn't guess.

"When the English first came, they swore they would live under the laws made by the West India Company," Kryn was saying. "If you don't know, this West India Company rules New Netherlands by permission of our Dutch government in the fatherland."

"I see," the boy said, but he didn't see.

Kryn said, "And then four years ago, what did our Director-General Stuyvesant do? He signed a paper with the English Governor Winthrop of Connecticut colony. He gave the colony all land east of this bay!" He snorted in disgust again. "No sense to it! Careful there."

While he talked, Kryn had helped the boy down a sandy slope to a tiny log dock. A round-bowed, wide sailboat bobbed close in to shore. The fishing shallop's sails were a faded red, and its bow partly covered to give some shelter from the weather. The boy had to climb over boxes and kegs of oyster shells to reach the bow of the shallop. Kryn tossed him a blanket and made ready to cast off quickly, for a wind had sprung up.

Just as they moved away, a black shadow rushed across the logs and leaped for the sailboat. At that moment the wind bellied the sails and the boat veered.

18

Splash! The dog missed and struck the water.

"Kryn," the boy called weakly. "Stop! It's my dog."

The dog was swimming, faster than any dog the boy had ever seen. Another moment and he was at the side of the boat.

"Ach, that dog! Not in here!" Kryn shouted back.

"Please. Help me," the boy begged. Forgetting his painful head, he leaned far over the side to seize the dog's front paw. Between the dog's frantic efforts to climb aboard and the boy's pulling, they did it at last. He crowded next to the boy and shook himself, spraying water.

"Ho!" chuckled the boy, who was kneeling on the slippery boards. "I've had enough of showers." He wiped his face on his sleeve then patted the dog's strong back. "He's almost dry here. He sheds water like a seal, or a sea lion."

He pulled the dog under the half-deck with him, away from the wind. He wrapped the blanket about both of them. "You'll let him stay, won't you, Kryn?"

"I'll not feed him," the oysterman warned, steering his shallop out into the Sound.

"I'll take care of him," the boy promised. He

19

didn't know how just yet, but he would do his best.

He lay back in the blanket, satisfied. "I think I'll call him Lion," he murmured. "You're strong as one, eh, Lion?" He rubbed the big dog's soft ear and felt Lion's warm tongue on his cheek.

After a while Kryn said, "Never saw that kind of dog before. Now that I think of it, I heard tell lately of a new breed from New Found Land in Canada. Seems it's a mixture of wolves and of dogs from the Old World ships fishing off the New Found Land Banks."

The boy whistled. How exciting that would be if Lion were truly a dog of the New World!

For several hours they scudded under a stiff breeze. Once a sail appeared to starboard, but faded away.

"Maybe it's our patrol boat on the lookout for that blasted English pirate, Thomas Baxter," Kryn said, his eyes on the fading sail.

"Pirates?" At that the boy pricked up his ears and opened his eyes. "Baxter?"

"*Ja*, yes. He's been capturing our Dutch trading sloops ever since the war began. Claims he has privateer papers given him by Rhode Island Plantation. Hides out in Connecticut ports, he does. He even takes English coastwise ships when he can.

20

Plain to see he uses the war as a thin excuse for piracy."

The boy wondered why he had begun to shake. Why should the name "Baxter" make him sweat?

"The Sound narrows here and becomes the East River," Kryn told him. On they sailed until they came to a dangerous rapids, where a smaller river flowed into the East River.

"We call this the Hellegat," Kryn shouted over the rush of waters. "This little river makes an island of the Manhattes, where New Amsterdam is."

It took all the fisherman's skill, the boy sensed, to shoot the boat past the small islands and rocks in the swirling current. Then they bounced into a narrow, deep current of water. "Only place deep enough to get through," Kryn flung out hurriedly.

After some tense moments the channel widened and the rocks were left behind. Kryn wiped his forehead with his canvas sleeve. The boy lay back and uncurled his fingers from Lion's coat.

"Could this be the only way to reach New Amsterdam?" he wondered aloud after a minute.

"*Ach*, no! Most ships go south of Long Island into the lower bay. Then they pass through the Narrows, between the two headlands of Staten Island and Long Island. From there they come out into the

21

upper bay, which is formed by the meeting of the East River and the great North River, as we call it. That's the one Hendrik Hudson discovered back in 1609. He called the land bordering it 'New Netherlands.'"

"Oh, I see. Will we be there soon?" the boy asked next, because the sun was fast setting.

"Soon enough," Kryn growled.

The boy could see a few farms in the clearings, surrounded by protecting log fences. The river narrowed suddenly and Kryn pointed out a farmhouse and boats tied before it. "The ferry to Breucklen over on Long Island." He waved his arm towards the high wooded shore across the river.

Near the ferry a windmill turned busily beside a warehouse and short dock at water's edge. "That's old Isaac Allerton's place," Kryn said next. "He's an English Puritan . . . came over on the ship *Mayflower*, he did, and has done well as a trader and merchant . . . has another place of business in Boston. He's always friendly to us Dutch. Gives me a fair price for my oysters, he does." Kryn added, "It was his sloop I was expecting."

The boy leaned forward eagerly as the little shallop came opposite a high stockade wall. It stretched, Kryn told him, from the small guardhouse on the shore a half-mile across the hilly island to Hendrik Hudson's river.

And clustered below that wall were the sharply pointed roofs of the town, cutting a saw-toothed pattern against the rosy sky.

A half-mile down at the tip of the island, the boy could make out the double gable and squat belltower of a church rising above the dirt walls of Fort Amsterdam. The church's slate roofs glistened in the sun. The orange, blue and white flag of the West India Company fluttered from a tall flagpole. West of the fort the arms of an ancient windmill moved slowly.

So this was Dutch New Amsterdam, one of the earliest settlements in the New World!

The boy swallowed hard, and he held Lion close. "What will we find here?" he whispered huskily to the dog. "Who are we, Lion?"

CHAPTER TWO

A Strange New World

KRYN THE OYSTERMAN shook the boy's shoulder the next morning. "Boy, wake up! Be on your way, you and your dog. It's sunrise."

"Huh? Where am I?" the boy mumbled sleepily. He sat up in Kryn's boat, careful of his sore head. He stretched his stiff arms. What a hard bed a boat made! Lion lay beside him, watching.

"We're at New Amsterdam. Beached at the trading place on the Graft, our little canal." Kryn waved his hand towards a ten-foot-wide ditch beside them. "We came late yesterday, can you remember?"

"Yes." Last night the boy had been too weak and tired to look about him much. He felt better now, and he did remember.

The little ditch seemed to run back through the town, with a few houses facing it. The tide was out,

24

and a strong smell of rotting timber and refuse struck the boy's nose.

Farmers had stationed their wagons and fisherfolk beached their boats around the wide, grassy trading place. Already they were moving about, arranging their wares for sale to the townspeople.

The boy stepped out of Kryn's boat. The rising sun brightened the row of brick warehouses and business places just south of him. They were built against each other, their gable ends toward the river road, their roofs notched back to a steep point. Each slate roof was topped by a rooster weather vane.

Last night before closing his eyes, the boy had thought that they somehow made him homesick for a Holland he couldn't recall. Beyond the houses he could see the grass-covered walls of little Fort Amsterdam.

Did Kryn say I should go there to report? The boy sighed. Surely I'll remember everything soon. I *must*, he told himself grimly. I have to know who I am and find my people . . . and find Lion's master.

The morning bells rang out. The noises around him grew as the town awoke. Geese and chickens cackled, dogs barked, cows mooed. Above him black and white sea gulls screeched and darted, hopeful of a free fish breakfast.

"Eat this." Kryn held out a half loaf of dark bread and a large chunk of cheese left over from their evening supper.

The boy took it hungrily. "Thank you, Kryn."

"When you're finished you can report to the Stadt Huis, the Town Hall." Kryn jerked his rusty head to the north across the Graft.

The boy looked up the river road beyond the canal, past a fenced corner garden, several houses, and empty lots. The Town Hall, which faced the water, must be the tallest building in town. He counted three stories with an attic in its steep roof. Atop it, he could see a belltower and flagpole.

"This year all strangers have to report to the town fathers," Kryn grumbled, and went back to carrying tubs of oysters from his boat.

The boy nodded silently and sat down on the ground. He broke off a big chunk of his bread, then looked to see if Kryn's back was turned.

"Catch, Lion," he said, and tossed the bread into Lion's open mouth. He laughed when the piece disappeared in one gulp. He patted Lion's head, and the dog licked his hand.

As they ate the boy watched a trading sloop anchored out in the river. A scow was being loaded from her. Across the wide river he saw the white sand bluffs of Long Island topped by pine forest. Far away on its north shore he had been shipwrecked. Was it only two days ago?

He pushed his yellow hair back from his face and gingerly touched his bandaged wound. The swollen cut had stopped hurting at last.

How I hate to go to the Town Hall alone and face strange men with my weak story, he thought.

He watched a stout woman in headband and full short skirts put a string of shell beads into Kryn's horny hand. Now that has to be the Wilden's seewan, or wampum, Kryn told me the people use for money here, he thought.

A bright-looking girl, about eleven, stood beside the woman. The boy caught her staring at him.

He stood up carefully. "Good-by, Kryn," he said, and to the dog, "Come along, Lion."

For a moment Lion didn't move.

"Can't you hear?" the boy cried impatiently.

He took a step and waved his hand. "Come," he said again.

This time Lion rose and came to him.

"Good morrow!" the girl said. Her pale blond hair was smoothed back into thick braids under a pretty quilted cap. Her blue eyes sparkled, and he could not help returning her friendly smile.

"You're new to me and I know all the children in town. What happened to your head? Where are you from, and what's your dog's name?" she said quickly.

She certainly can ask questions, the boy thought. Girls were taught to be more modest in Holland.

"Can't you speak?" the girl demanded.

He saw her look over his torn wool doublet and wide breeches, streaked with salt from the sea water. He wriggled his toes in the old wooden shoes Kryn had given him, and said nothing.

"Your clothes aren't leather or canvas, so you're not a fisherman's boy," she went on. "The oyster-

man says you were shipwrecked out east on the Sound near Oyster Bay. And you don't even remember your name," she declared in triumph. "Where are the others on your ship? Nobody here has heard of a shipwreck."

The boy felt his face grow hot. *Ach hemel*, what a girl! "No?" he said crossly. He turned away, mumbling, "I'm going to see the town officers. Maybe they will help me find out something."

The girl's rosy face looked sad for a moment. "Please don't be angry. I suppose I chatter too much. I'm sorry about your head and your bad luck. I hope you learn what happened to your people." She smiled sweetly at him. "My name is Anneke van der Grift. My father's a town alderman, a schepen, so I know they don't go to the courtrooms until nine o'clock."

"Thanks. I'll wait," he said shortly.

"But you will find work, to be sure," Anneke told him. "Servants and workers are scarce in our colony."

A low whistle sounded behind them. It came from a tall, thin boy carrying a woven Indian basket.

"Oh, good morrow, Hans Kregier," Anneke called out to him.

"And a good morrow to you, Annie," Hans replied, making a little bow. He glanced sharply at the boy.

Anneke stepped over to Hans and began to talk fast. She's telling him all she knows about me, the boy thought in disgust. He leaned over Lion and tied a light rope of Kryn's around his neck. He'd have to use one if Lion didn't obey.

Now he saw the oysterman coming toward him with a frown.

"I'm going, I'm going," the boy said hastily. He started to walk along the canal bank road to a bridge he saw a short way inland.

A breeze sprang up and blew puffs of dust ahead of him as he left the trading place. He had just passed the corner inn with the thatched roof, which faced the canal and the marketplace, when he heard Anneke call.

She caught up with him and said, out of breath, "Hans Kregier says that maybe his father can give you lodging for your services in his public house, or on his North River trading sloop. Hans is going home to ask his father now."

"Anneke, Ann-ne-ke!" the stout woman shouted after them. "What a worrisome maid!"

Anneke put her fingers over her red lips and giggled. "O-oo-oh, I forgot!" She rolled her eyes.

30

"Lintie and I have another errand to do. But I'm going to ask Mother if she can use you on the farm or at our house while my father is away. So please wait until you hear from us before you take work. Promise!"

Before the boy could answer she dashed back to the servant woman, Lintie. She really runs fast for a girl, he had to admit. But her offer of help probably doesn't mean much, he thought.

He walked on, wondering if he would meet someone who knew him or Lion. He saw Hans Kregier waiting at the canal bridge.

The lanky Hans wore a good green doublet with slashed sleeves, darker green wide breeches, and leather shoes with buckles. Under his wide brimmed hat, his light brown hair reached almost to his shoulders, just as the boy's did.

"Where are you going?" Hans said, and leaned back against the bridge rail to avoid a man leading an oxcart.

"Since all strangers have to report to Town Hall, that's where I'm going," the boy said.

Hans nodded. "It's up the road a way . . . you can see it. Try to avoid talking to Schout-Fiscal Van Ten, our sheriff. He's General Stuyvesant's right-hand man and a terror. Instead, ask for the town clerk."

"I will." The boy touched his sore head. It was aching again.

"You ought to have a surgeon look at that," Hans remarked. "But then, you have no money. Anneke van der Grift's father sailed for the West Indies last month as skipper of the *Dolphin*, a company ship. So he can't help you. He owns one of the big warehouses there along the river." Hans stopped talking a moment and bit his lip thoughtfully. "I'm going to ask my father to help you."

"That's kind of you." The boy smiled at him. Hans seemed to want to be friendly. "There's one thing, though. I won't leave Lion here to starve. He has to come along with me, too. Unless—" he hated to think about it— "unless he finds his master."

Hans looked troubled at that. "I . . . I don't know about the dog. Our housekeeper hates them. And I hate her! She has a nasty temper. My mother died last year." Hans put out his hand and stroked Lion's broad head, as if to show that *he* liked dogs. "I'll see," he said before he started away. "I live across the fort's parade grounds on the North River."

How kind he and the girl are to a stranger, the boy thought as he followed a fat burgher across the bridge. On the other side he went along a footpath that edged the canal and a large fenced-in garden.

Just as he turned the corner of the fence and back into the river road, the fence gate opened. A short fat man stepped out in front of the boy and Lion.

At the same instant a strong gust of wind blew dust in the boy's eyes. He dropped Lion's rope. Then he heard roars of rage as he wiped his burning eyes.

"Stop that beast! *Hemel!* he's got my beaver hat. Catch him," the fat man screamed.

The boy stood frozen to the spot. The man hopped about after Lion. The dog's face was almost covered by the curling plumes which trimmed the hat he carried in his mouth. This didn't keep him from staying just out of the angry man's reach. Lion

pranced back and forth, delighted with the play.

"Dirck, oh Dirck!" whooped the fat man.

"Yes, Mynheer," the boy answered before he thought. He stepped forward. At the same time a servant started to come through the gate.

The fat man whirled about and glared at the boy. His tiny mustache and pointed beard quivered on his red, swollen face. "I'm calling my servant, Dirck," he shouted. "Who are you? Are you a Dirck? And is this your rascal dog?"

"Yes, Mynheer," the boy replied. Then his heart did a flip-flop. What was he saying? Was it his name? He had answered to it naturally. Suddenly he felt sure that his name really was Dirck. He decided he would use it, come what might.

Maybe I'll soon remember more, he thought excitedly.

Then he heard the stout man still shouting at him. "Stop that dog before he ruins my beaver hat. Else I'll throw you both in jail."

CHAPTER THREE

A New Master

DIRCK STOOD THERE on that strange road in a strange town, and he was frightened by the man's angry words. He could see he meant business. Jail!

"Come here, Lion," he ordered. But Lion only lay down in the dust and held onto the hat. He slowly waved his long tail to show he was having a wonderful time. U. S. 1187798

"Come here!" Dirck repeated louder.

"The dog's stupid," the fat man snorted. "Where's a stick?"

Dirck frowned. He ran quickly forward, snatched up the end of Lion's rope and pulled hard. "Come!"

Lion got up and came toward Dirck. He hung his head, the hat's feather trailing in the dust.

"You must learn to come when I call you," Dirck told him sternly.

35

Lion looked up with puzzled brown eyes. Dirck almost smiled, for the dog looked so funny with the feather curling around his head. Taking the large hat from Lion's mouth, he brushed it off as best he could. He gave it to the angry man with a bow. "I'm very sorry, Your Worship."

"Young man, if you have forgotten . . . I'm Cornelis Van Ten. I'm the town sheriff, the schout-fiscal. I'm also sheriff for the whole colony of New Netherlands. So you and your bad dog had better stay out of my way," the schout blustered. "Where do you dwell, and who are your parents?"

"I . . . I can't remember," Dirck stammered.

"Can't remember?" the sheriff sputtered. "*Ach*, are you a Dirck NoName?" He stamped his booted foot. "Don't make sport of me!"

Dirck explained what had happened to him as best he could.

Cornelis Van Ten eyed him coldly and pulled at his reddish mustaches. "Hmph! Strange! We've had no reports of a ship lost in the storm," he said. "But our ship on patrol against the pirates in Long Island Sound is due back. Come along to the Town Hall with me. We will have to make a report of this. Guard well that wicked dog, Dirck NoName, or out he goes into the river!"

Dirck followed the strutting Van Ten and his servant up the street. They soon came to the Town Hall's large garden. It reached back to the next lane, called Hoogh, and was entirely fenced in.

The shore in front of the square building had been newly planked up and filled in with dirt and stone. Dirck saw that workmen were building a plank wall on down the river shore toward the canal to protect it against being washed away by the tide. The Town Hall used to be the Town Inn, Kryn had told Dirck. But the little village of New Amsterdam changed that last year, in 1653, when it officially became a city.

When they stepped into the wide entrance hall, Dirck saw a number of leather firebuckets hanging on one wall, ready to be used in case of a fire. He followed Schout Van Ten into a small side office. There he told the secretary of the town council, Jacob Kip, the little that he knew about himself.

The sheriff ordered the bells on the roof rung three times. Then he sent old Teunis Kraey, the town crier, to call the people before the Town Hall. A group of curious citizens soon gathered. Dirck and Lion were pushed onto a wooden platform standing in front of the building.

The sheriff told the people Dirck's story. "Does

anyone know this boy or the black dog?" He looked about. "No? Then, until the boy recovers his wits or we hear news of his ship and people, we will have to care for him. He can work for his bed and food. The cut on his head seems to be healing well, and he is sturdy enough. If someone will offer to take Dirck NoName for a while, I can get on with more important work."

"Ho! ho!" The words came from a boy who stood in the rear with a group of children. "What work?" he jeered.

A few people giggled, then there was silence.

Dirck moved his feet uneasily. He felt odd, standing there before all those pairs of eyes. He suddenly knew that they were unfriendly eyes . . . for him or for Van Ten?

"Enough of this nonsense." The sheriff glared angrily. "Come come, who offers?"

The people glared back at him. At last a round farmer raised his hand. "I can use the lad on my farm across the North River," he said.

Dirck asked, "And my dog? I can't leave him."

"No, no!" the farmer said. "We have too many dogs to feed on our bouwerie, our farm. Besides, I won't take a wicked pirate dog."

Dirck's cheeks burned, and he threw his arms

about Lion's neck. "He's no pirate dog! And I'll not go without him," he said fiercely.

"Why do you call him a pirate dog?" the sheriff demanded, scowling.

Another Dutchman, who carried a long clay pipe, spoke up. "Our patrol ship has just docked, Your Worship. The soldiers say they saw floating wreckage near Eaton's Neck and part of a flag with Rhode Island's colors. We all know that Rhode Island has given sea pirates permission to capture our shipping under her flag. If this dog and boy came from such a ship, well—" he glanced around the crowd— "we might have here a cabin boy and dog who belong to one of those pirates. Maybe someone taught this boy to speak Dutch. Maybe he's a spy!" He puffed excitedly on his pipe.

Dirck could see everyone nod his head. His heart sank and his head began to ache again. I'll never find a place, he thought dismally.

A thin man with a face like a knife stepped forward. "Sam Low's my name, Your Worship. I'll take the boy." His voice cracked like gravel. "I need help in my store. But he must be quick. I'll teach him that, I vow!" He twisted his lips in a pretended smile.

Dirck stared at him with a feeling of instant dislike. He took a deep breath and forced himself to say, "Will you take my dog, sir?"

Sam Low rubbed his sharp nose. "I care not. Keep him from underfoot. Is it settled, Schout Van Ten?"

"Good and done! Good and done!" Van Ten slapped the silver sword hanging at his side. He ordered Dirck, "Go along with Sam Low for now, Dirck NoName. Be close at hand, in case we hear anything." He stepped down from the platform.

Dirck and Lion followed Sam Low through the unfriendly crowd. He tried to see Anneke or Hans among the group of children, but did not. He felt a sharp pinch on his arm and looked around. A moonfaced boy laughed at him.

"Dirck NoName! Ho, ho!" the boy said softly. None of the others smiled at Dirck.

He clenched his fists but walked on after Sam Low. He stared curiously as he passed two Wilden, who stood near their dugout canoe pulled up on the riverbank. A narrow strip of bristling black hair topped each of their shaven heads. A red deer hair ornament was fastened to the bristles. Copper earrings swung from their ears, and scarves of plaid duffel trade cloth were draped over their right shoulders. At their feet lay bundles of beaver skins.

40

They came here to the island to trade their furs, Dirck thought. These were the red men from across Hudson's River, from inland. They looked fierce, and he would not like to be alone with them.

He saw Sam Low barely nod to the Wilden as he passed. Then Sam stopped and said, "Turn here at the fence corner and walk up this side of the canal. Go past the Hoogh Street bridge and on up to the next lane. That will be the Slyck Steegh, Mud Lane. My store is on the corner by the canal. The only other place on the lane is the Bark Mill. Long Mary, my housekeeper, will be there."

Dirck started to follow the path back along the canal. It lay beside the house and garden where he first met the sheriff. He felt someone clutch his arm. It was Anneke again!

"S-s-sh!" she said before he could open his mouth. "I don't want that nasty Sam Low to hear us. I just heard you are to work in his old store," she complained. "And after I got Mother's permission for you to help at our warehouse and also at our farm. Oh, why didn't you wait? I hurried as fast as I could."

"I'm sorry," Dirck said. He flushed. "I thought you might not come back or want to bother with me. And I had to make sure I could keep Lion. Nobody wanted him."

Oh, why had he been so impatient? Now he had lost a good home for himself and Lion. "I'm truly sorry," he said again.

"*Ach!*" Anneke made a little face. "You promised to wait. Now you'll have a miserable time. Sam Low is not a nice man."

"He reminds me of a weasel with his slippery look," Dirck admitted.

"People say he's not honest," Anneke told him. "They suspect he tries a little fur and tobacco smuggling on the side. That's to escape paying duties on them to the West India Company. It has charge of all trade going in or out of here, you know." She glanced over her shoulder at Sam Low, who was standing near the Indians now. "Why can't you just come home with me?"

Dirck shook his head sorrowfully. "I can't without asking the sheriff to agree to it. And he won't bother to help me more, since he's angry about Lion and his hat." He told her about Lion's playful trick, and she laughed.

"So you remember your name is Dirck? That's good! You'll remember more, just wait."

"I hope so. There's another thing," he went on. "Would your mother want to take in a pirate dog or an English spy?"

42

"Pray, what do you mean?" Anneke demanded. "Lion doesn't look like a pirate. He's a dog!" She threw back her head and laughed so merrily that she made Dirck chuckle, too.

"That's so," he said. "And I can speak a bit of English . . . where I learned it, I don't know. The townsfolk think that Lion *might* have been on a pirate ship which *might* have sunk in the gale. Me, too. That's a silly idea." He tried to ignore the fear in his heart.

Anneke nodded. "Everyone's so very suspicious now. We're afraid the New England Colonies might attack us, and we are few compared to them. Not more than a thousand here in New Amsterdam, and only ten thousand in all New Netherlands. My father has sailed away to get—"

"I think my new master is coming this way," Dirck said quickly. "Many thanks, Anneke. You're the only kind person I've met in this town, oh, and maybe Hans." He pushed her off ahead of him.

He watched her run swiftly along the side of the little canal, her red quilted overskirt belling out over her many petticoats. She crossed the bridge at Hoogh Street, which led down to the north wall of the Fort. She was soon lost to sight among the people, horses and oxcarts.

43

He and Lion followed the canal path. A few rowboats were tied to rotting timbers which braced the sides of the ditch here and there. At the bridge he stopped to look to his right up Hoogh Street, the opposite way Anneke had taken. He saw that some new stone and brick houses stood among the older wood ones with reed roofs. Farther up he could see that the road passed the back entrance to the Town Hall garden before it curved down to meet the river road.

He walked on. Just ahead was an old reed-thatched cottage at the corner of a narrow lane.

"That's it!" he exclaimed.

Beside the doorway hung a broken sign with a large ear of Indian corn painted on it, and beneath was a name, "Low, Trader." A window near the divided Dutch door was covered with dirty greased paper.

Dirck kicked a rooting pig out of the muddy path and stepped inside.

CHAPTER FOUR

Anneke Again

TWO DAYS LATER Dirck slipped a wooden water-bucket carrier from his shoulders. He leaned the yoke against the outside kitchen wall of Sam Low's cottage. Then, kicking open the door, he carried two buckets of water inside and set them upon the sanded floor.

"Here's your water, Long Mary," he said to Sam Low's housekeeper. Once each day he had to carry water from the well near the fort to the cottage.

"Aye, that's the one thing you remembered to do." Long Mary sniffed.

With a sigh, Dirck sat down on a stool and stretched his legs toward the supper fire. He gently tugged at Lion's ears while he said to Long Mary, "I wonder where the master goes on his mysterious errands."

45

Long Mary recited to him:

"If ye stick your thumb where it doesn't belong,
The world will yank it good and strong."

Dirck stared at her. She was almost six feet tall, with a face like a witch's. He frowned and said slowly, "You mean I shouldn't ask any questions."

"It's taking a chance, ye are, with that sly man! He's let ye be so far, but mark me! He's beat all his former bondservants, and he'll treat ye the same, should you get too curious," Long Mary warned.

"Is that why they ran away?" Dirck said. "By a whale's flippers, I've worked in the store since cock-crow. I've tried to clean the place and serve the few customers he's had. I want to please him so I can keep Lion with me. But the master's not even been near me or the store."

"Aye, but don't ever ask what he's about," the housekeeper warned again.

Long Mary had come from Salem in the Massachusetts Bay Colony years ago, she had told Dirck. "When my mistress hung a round glass witch ball by the door, I knew it was time to leave," she said. "There was talk of the burning of witches. Some of those Puritans whispered that I was a witch, just because I knew my herbs and simples better than

46

the others. Purslan, pennyroyal, snakeroot, and balsam of bats. He, he!" She had jerked at the old-fashioned soiled ruff around her neck. "So I disappeared. In a clap of thunder! He, he!" She had squinted down her long nose at Dirck and he had felt gooseflesh on his arms.

Dirck did not like this dark kitchen. Dusty cobwebs swung in the corners of the low, beamed ceiling, which was black with smoke. The usual Dutch cupboard-bed, the betse, was built into the wall opposite the fireplace. One of its doors hung from a broken hinge, so that inside he could see Sam Low's soiled feather bed. A rough, square table, two rush-bottomed chairs, benches, old chests, and some shelves for mugs and dishes completed the room.

Last night he had tossed on his own straw pallet in the loft under the thatched roof. From the rustlings and squealing he guessed that there were bats as well as rats in the loft. Yet what had kept him awake were the questions rolling inside his bruised head.

Where were his parents, if he had any? And who owned Lion? If only he could remember! He beat his fists against the straw. Then and there he decided that he would try to seek out Director-General Stuyvesant in spite of Sam Low or Sheriff Van Ten.

So now he stood up in the kitchen and kicked his stool aside. "I have need of some air, Long Mary. Would I dare to walk out and see the town? It's an hour to sundown," he said. "My head feels better, too, thanks to your herbs . . . or is it witchcraft?" He gave her a wink. No need to say he hoped to find General Stuyvesant.

Long Mary pushed a strand of gray hair back under her dirty cap. She shrugged. "Humph! He who talks most, knows the least. It's your care to be back before your master returns and finds you gone. I expect him at sundown."

"I'll be back in time," he promised hastily. "I'll take Lion. He's out in back."

He went to the door of the kitchen lean-to and called out. "Come, Lion."

Lion knew his name now and always came when called. But this time the dog didn't come bounding across Long Mary's young tulips and herb plants. He was nowhere inside the fenced-in yard!

Dirck burst into the kitchen. "Lion's gone!" he shouted to Long Mary. "I've got to find him. He must have jumped over the fence where it's falling down."

Long Mary cackled. "Last I sighted him he was watching a cat walk along the fence top."

Dirck stepped into the foreroom which Sam Low used as his store. He snatched a cord from a shelf. He needed it as a leash in case he caught Lion. He simply had to find his dog at once. His call on General Stuyvesant would have to wait.

Outside on the corner he glanced up and down the canal and the lane. Should he cross the footbridge and cut over to the plain before the fort, or should he head toward the East River road? He'd try the river front where he and Lion first landed, he decided.

At the river he cut across the trading place, empty today, and turned right toward the row of business houses. He could not find Lion. He was afraid to call out, for the people might notice him more.

He brushed past a housevrouw carrying a goose in a basket. She stared at him. Maybe he did look funny in his canvas sailor's breeches and old velvet jerkin. Long Mary had found them for him while she mended his own clothes.

Scraps of French and English words came to his ears as he hurried past groups of sailors and traders standing about the streets. Not as many as before the trouble with England, when trade was booming, Long Mary had told him.

The first brick warehouse he passed had Sheriff

Van Ten's name on it. The West India Company's initials were over the wide open door of the next warehouse. From it came the strong odor of dried tobacco leaf and fur pelts, stamped and packed for the next boat for Holland.

Two coastal sloops bobbed out in the river. He saw a scow being loaded at the short dock on the landing place at Schreyer's Hook just below. He made sure that Lion was not swimming in the water.

As Dirck came to the third warehouse he read the name "Van der Grift" on a sign beside the wide door. That was Anneke's last name. He looked inside.

Farm and ship supplies crowded bales of fur pelts, tobacco and stacks of lumber. A farmer in red leather coat and breeches was trading for a wood ox yoke. Sacks of grain lay at his feet.

Dirck set his lip and hurried on. Lion, where are you? he thought almost angrily. He knew that if he lost Lion, it would be a hard thing to bear on top of all else that had happened. A growing dread filled him. Could the dog's real master have found him?

When he reached the corner of the fort, he turned west up the Marckveldt Road. It ran slightly uphill along the north wall to meet the plain, or green, before the fort. Neat, fenced gardens and houses faced the dirt road. Wood benches were built on

50

each side of the house entrances, and brass knockers shone on each door.

"Stay, Dirck NoName!"

He whirled about. It was Anneke. She was out of breath, and her pretty lace cap had slipped a little over one ear. She took a deep breath. "Mother and I were calling on Surgeon Kierstede's family, and I ran out when I saw you pass."

Anneke glanced at his head. "You should have had the surgeon stitch up your cut. Tell me, do you recall anything more?"

"No." Dirck shook his head glumly. "Only my name. My cut is healing, although the lump's still there. I don't even need a bandage . . . Long Mary fixed it up."

"*Ach*, that witch!" Anneke wrinkled her nose, then laughed. "Oh! I've been wondering if you were still safe," she went on in a lower voice. "There are more stories about your Sam Low. They say that one of those English pirates, Thomas Baxter, stole Jan Caspar's sloop. The wicked thief! And he robbed Will Harck a few months ago. Both men swear that Sam Low was back of it. Others claim that the pirate and his crew were seen creeping out of Sam's house one night, and he denies it. Mevrouw Kierstede was just telling Mother."

Dirck nodded. "Maybe so. But I haven't time to talk now, Anneke. I'm looking for Lion. He's loose somewhere. I don't want anyone to take him to the sheriff."

Suddenly Anneke began to hop up and down, pointing over his shoulder. "There he is, look! He just ran across the road. He's headed for the sally-port of the fort."

Dirck started to run. His dog had disappeared beyond the next corner of the fort. Dirck dashed around into the plain. And there was Lion with another dog, drinking at the wooden water trough beside the town well!

"Lion!" Dirck called hoarsely. The dog looked up, his jaws dripping, and gave a whine of delight. He loped over to Dirck.

With a rush of relief, Dirck knelt and put his arms tightly about Lion's middle. "You rascal," he said happily, and rubbed his face in the warm fur. "What a shock you gave me, running away like that."

"Woof, woof," Lion replied in his deep voice, and he licked Dirck's nose.

Dirck turned to smile at Anneke, who had followed him. "Thanks for helping me find him. You're bright for a girl."

Anneke laughed. "*Ach*, Father says girls are

smarter. Father says . . ." She stopped and smoothed down her samare, the long, loose jacket she was wearing. When she looked up, tears brimmed over her china-blue eyes. "I told you that Father sailed far south to the West Indies Islands. He took a load of lumber and hard bread. He's on an important errand for our Director-General Stuyvesant, because he's to bring back powder . . ." She caught her breath and bit her lip. "Oh, I'm not to tell," she added.

Dirck stood up and gave her arm an awkward pat. "Don't worry. I'm very sorry your father had to go, when he seems to do a good business here. He must be a very good skipper."

Anneke lifted her round chin proudly. "He's a brave skipper of the *Dolphin*, and a good business man. He's worked hard. He came here from Amsterdam with General Stuyvesant in 1647, when I was almost five. He started as a company clerk. Dirck, we expect him back now. Will you help me watch for his ship?"

"I will, if I'm still here," Dirck said thoughtfully. "I'm not sure that I like this New World, or the people here." Strange . . . he had the feeling that once he had wanted very much to come.

Her cheeks turned bright pink at his words. "Indeed, Dirck NoName! You have no choice but to stay here until that silly mind of yours works again. No one asked you to come."

She started to walk away, swishing her full skirts angrily.

Dirck hurried after her. Just like a girl, he thought. But she was his only friend. "Please don't be angry," he said. "I didn't mean you. See, Lion's sorry, too."

Anneke looked down at Lion. The dog pushed against her, raising his sorrowful brown eyes. He made a funny little noise.

"*Ach*, what a dog!" She laughed and began to stroke his back. "We are friends again."

"Tell me," Dirck urged, "do you know if the sheriff has learned anything more about the shipwreck out in Long Island Sound?"

"No, not yet." Anneke shook her head. "It takes a while for news to travel."

Dirck squared his shoulders and watched a group of men march into the sally-port of the fort. "Then I'm going to brave the Director-General himself. Maybe he can help me find my home."

"You can't see him, Dirck. He's gone up the North River to Fort Orange. That's one hundred and fifty miles north of here."

Disappointed, Dirck kicked at a stone in the dust.

54

"Have to do something," he muttered fiercely. "I can't go on, not knowing . . ."

"Yes," Anneke said. "We'll think of a plan soon. Only, while we're here, don't you want to see our fort?"

He hesitated and glanced at the lowering sun in the blue April sky. "I have to be back at sundown," he began.

"Oh come, it will take just a minute. And I'd like to show you more of our city in the wilderness," she told him.

"Hardly big enough to be a real city," Dirck retorted with a smile. "Only a half a mile long and half a mile at its widest, and not one cobblestone paved road to its name."

"It's the best town in the New World," Anneke said stoutly. "Better than New Plymouth, or New Boston, or Virginia."

Dirck walked over toward the stone-lined entrance to the fort. The double log doors stood open. "This old fort looks as if it isn't much good," he declared. "Half the log palisade fence is gone from the outside. Long Mary says the hogs root in the earth ramparts, and that horses and goats eat the sod."

"Yes." She sighed. "We have a law now that says all yards are to be fenced to keep in the animals.

We have a town herdsman, too, who takes the cows outside the wall to the commons. But some people just don't care. They take the log palisades away to use as firewood."

She leaned down and stroked Lion's head. "Although, the whole town did help to build our wall last summer. They helped to pay for it, too. It goes clear across the island from the East River to Hudson's River, which we usually call the North River. I suppose you've seen the two gates; one's at the Strand, our river road, and the other's at the end of Heere Street, over the hill there." She waved her hand toward a wide road which led north from the green up and over a steep little hill. "I live—"

"How much good will the wall be," Dirck interrupted, "when the town is open to both rivers?"

"The wall will protect us in case the English or Wilden attack, goose! There's a war in Europe, you know," she told him.

Dirck raised his eyebrows and shook his mussed yellow hair. He went closer to the gate entrance, where he could watch the soldiers, workmen and Company slaves move in and out of the fort.

"What's that?" He pointed inside to a large brick building.

"That's General Stuyvesant's house. He's going

to build a fine new one next to the landing place on the East River. The big stone church with a double roof is Saint Nicholas'. Over on the other side are the barracks, jailhouse and storehouses. Only we have very little powder and lead to store," she added.

The marching men wheeled and came toward Dirck and Anneke at the entrance. They stepped back.

"Those men are part of our citizen, our burgher, guard," she said as the guard passed them and lined up on the green. "The West India Company never sent us more soldiers, as they promised to do. So we started a citizen's militia last year when we officially became a city with our own Council. That Captain drilling the men is Hans's father, Burgomaster Martin Kregier."

A strong-looking man in steel breastplate and helmet fiercely shouted orders to the awkward militia. Suddenly he gave a final order, the men broke ranks, and the Captain strode toward a group of three houses at the far side of the green. Dirck noticed that the few houses on that side of the green and the wide road were made of brick, whereas those on this side of Heere Street were small wood cottages.

"The tall house in the middle is the Kregier Inn," Anneke explained. "Mynheer Kregier also owns a

57

river sloop, the *Sea Mew*. He uses it for the Wilden trade upriver. He wants Hans to learn to be a soldier and fur trader, but Hans doesn't like the idea."

"That's too bad. I'm sorry, Anneke, but I have to go back now," Dirck said. "Come along, Lion." He pulled at the cord he'd tied about the dog's neck.

Anneke smiled. "I'd better go home, too."

"Where do you live, Anneke?"

"I tried to tell you before. Right up Heere Street, past the hill a piece." She waved her hand to the north. "It's the widest street in town and follows the North River. Our garden ends at the river shore bluffs. We're next to the burying place."

"Ugh!" Dirck pretended to shiver. "A pleasant place to live!"

But she only smiled, refusing to be teased. "Outside the wall the road's called the Breede Weg and goes to the 'Flat,' our common pasture for the town's cows and goats." Then she caught the sleeve of his jacket. "Do wait one more little moment. I've thought of my favorite place I want to show you. Please," she coaxed.

Dirck cast an anxious glance at the sun, low in the west. "I can't."

"It's not far. Just past the old windmill," she begged.

58

The windmill stood on a knoll between the fort's west wall and the North River. Its large sails barely moved.

"Our mill grinds the grain from the Company's farms outside the wall," Anneke said. "People claim that the Wilden are afraid of our windmills, because of the big sails and the 'stone teeth' that grind our grain."

Dirck laughed at that. Anneke showed him the path between the mill and a large house on the corner next to the inn. They stopped under a locust tree and gazed out over the wide stretch of water. For here the mighty Hudson's River joined the East River in a vast bay.

The sky's blue melted into pink and red and purple. The rim of the green forest on the bluffs across the two-mile wide river looked far away to Dirck. A canoe of woodsrunners, "bossenloopers," and a log canoe of Wilden hurried back to camp.

On the bay hundreds of wild geese and noisy swans floated like a white island. The breeze seemed soft, carrying the tang of salt and fish.

Dirck swallowed, and after a moment he said, "It makes one feel small . . . and . . . and lonesome."

Anneke flashed him an understanding look. "It does, but I love it."

The tinkling of cow bells rippled out on the air. Dogs barked and cattle lowed. Lion, quiet until now, pricked up his big soft ears. "Woof!" he warned.

"That's Gabriel, the herdsman! He's bringing all the cows home from the Flat," Anneke exclaimed. "It's almost time for supper."

"And it's past time for me to get back before my master," Dirck answered. "I'll see more of the town later. My thanks, and a good-day to you."

He walked swiftly back to the green. Everyone seemed to have gone home. He saw a herd of cows, sheep and goats coming toward him down Heere Street. The old herdsman blew his horn in front of each of the cottages that lined the other side of the wide road. Then a child came out to open the gate for the family cow to enter. By the time Dirck and Lion ran across the green, they met the herd and had to wait for it to pass.

All at once shrill yells rang out. "Ouitchke, ouitchke-e-e-e! It's the Wilden!" Then Indian arrows came whizzing over the backs of the animals from the Beaver Path, another of the narrow lanes which led into the plain.

Was this a Wilden attack? Dirck's heart jumped. Lion barked excitedly and pulled at his cord. Now

60

several boys, yelling and dancing about, followed the arrows.

A fat boy carried a small bow. Behind him ran a large animal which looked more wolf than dog.

Old Gabriel, the herdsman, shook a long staff he carried. "Begone! Wilden dogs!" he shouted. "You, Goosen, stop your tricks or I'll tell the sheriff." He swung his staff in a circle at the hooting boys.

They ducked. But in the scramble someone stumbled over the wolf-dog. Dirck heard a cry, then a snarl. Lion chose this moment to jump playfully into the group.

CHAPTER FIVE

Errand by Night

DIRCK GASPED when the dog's cord jerked from his fingers. "Lion!" he cried.

In a flash the wolf-dog turned on Lion. The two animals rolled over and over in the dust, snapping and growling at each other.

Anneke ran back down the Heere Street hill. "Stop them," she shrieked.

"Stop, ye Wilden," shouted old Gabriel at the fighting dogs. With a final swing of his long staff, the herdsman urged his frightened flock on to the next houses around the bend in the road.

"I'll not forget this," he called over his shoulder. "I'll report you to the Town Council."

Goosen, the fat boy, lay howling on the ground. Dirck and three other boys separated the dogs with the aid of a stick and a bucket of water from the well.

At that, Goosen's dog snarled and slunk limping away.

Dirck anxiously looked over Lion. The panting dog stood still with his eyes fixed on Dirck.

Finally Dirck said, "He's all right, but for this slight cut in his ear. *Ach,* I'm surprised at you, Lion!" He looked up at the circle of boys and Anneke. "He seemed so good-natured."

"That black imp bit my leg," Goosen cried, and his fat cheeks quivered. He sat up in the dust. His tan hair, like coarse rope, stuck out in all directions.

"Your dog started to fight Lion," Dirck said stoutly. "Maybe he bit you."

"Roelf's wild enough to do so," one of the boys said to Dirck. "It wouldn't be the first time."

Goosen held his leg and shouted, "My dog Roelf didn't bite me. Look!" A small circle of blood was staining his knit stocking. "Your old pirate dog did it."

Dirck set his jaw. "Don't say that again," he said in a low, fierce tone. "Lion's no pirate dog. Come along, Lion," he ordered, the cord in his hand. He knew if he fought Goosen he might get into more trouble.

"Pirate dog!" Goosen spit out the taunt.

At these words, Dirck whirled and ran over to the

town well. Quickly he filled the bucket there and brought it back. Before the fat boy knew what was happening, Dirck had turned the bucket of water over Goosen's head.

"Ye-ow!" Goosen shrieked. "Stop it!" Dripping water, he struggled to his feet. He spluttered, "I'll turn Roelf on you for that! I'll tell the Town Council."

Dirck walked away quietly to the laughter of the other boys. Maybe later he would be ashamed of his trick, but right now he felt good! No one was going to insult Lion.

Anneke caught up with him, full of giggles. "Serves him right," she declared. "That Goosen is a round ball of wickedness. He's often been called up before my father and the other councilmen because of his pranks. Don't be cast down about what he will do."

Dirck smiled at her. "Oh, I'm not. Bullies are cowards at heart. He won't do anything." He started to laugh at the thought of Goosen rolling along like a ball. Then he stopped, for he saw the last glowing streaks of the setting sun. "It's getting dark, and I have to go back to the store as fast as I can. I must be there before Sam Low returns tonight."

Would he get there in time? He wet his lips and turned into a narrow lane that cut over to the canal. Anneke still trotted at his heels. Lion loped on ahead, his strong muscles moving smoothly under his shining coat. He seemed none the worse for his fight.

Suddenly Dirck heard a voice calling out, "Hear ye! Hear ye! Citizens, come gather at the Town Hall. A placard against Thomas Baxter, the English pirate, is to be read. A fine reward for his capture. Hear ye, hear ye!"

It was Teunis Kraey, the town crier, ringing his bell in the next lane.

A cold fear caught at Dirck's throat. Thomas Baxter! That name again. Why, he wondered, did the pirate's name frighten him?

Now he wished he could join the people who gathered at the Town Hall. He turned to Anneke with a sudden idea.

"Could you get the news at the Town Hall for me? I can't stop along the way."

Anneke shook her head and tugged at her white cap. "I'm sorry. I'll have to leave you here, Dirck. Old Mistress Lintie will box my ears if I'm late for her supper. But I can find out what it's all about for you. And I'll think of some way to bring her to your store. Good night, Dirck."

She smiled and was gone. It was a good thing to have a friend in this strange, unfriendly land! Then he started to run.

When he slipped through the Dutch door of Sam's cottage, Long Mary stood in the doorway between the store and the kitchen.

"The master?" Dirck whispered, out of breath. She didn't answer, merely shook her head and returned to her cook-fire.

No one else was in the place. Dirck breathed easier. He took a small money box from the shelf and counted the few strings and beads of black and white seewan he had taken in. Then he joined Long Mary by the fire in the dusk.

The next day he was surprised to see Hans Kregier come into the store. "Good morrow, Dirck No-Name." Hans grinned at him. "I bring a message."

"And what is it, Hans HaveaName?" Dirck returned his grin. He felt better this morning. The lump on his head was gone and the cut almost closed. If only his memory would heal as quickly!

"'Tis this: Anneke is kept abed with a sore throat. But she says that you must still hope. She seems to be plotting to carry you off to their bouwerie, their farm, a few miles north of town."

Dirck smiled regretfully. "She is a kind maid, but

I would make a poor farm helper. In fact, I think I don't know how to do much of anything."

"Never too late to learn, as Long Mary says." Hans gazed into space. "'Tis odd, but I want to keep on learning . . . much more than the simple things I learned at our little public school. I want to know more about our New Netherland's wild life: more about the Maquas, whom the English call Mohawks, and the other tribes. By Saint Nicholas, I could go north to Fort Orange on my father's river sloop, then west to Maquas country . . ." He shrugged, and the eager light died in his gray eyes.

"Then why don't you?" Dirck said. "I'd never care to, but you're fifteen, aren't you? Almost a man."

Hans nodded. "Just the same, my father thinks of me as a small lad." He flushed. "I haven't had a chance to talk to him about you."

He turned away and stumbled over a firkin of shelled corn. At the door he stopped. "Saint Nicholas! Annie said this was most important, and I near forgot. There's a reward posted at the Town Hall for the capture of any pirates. One hundred guilders apiece."

Dirck whistled.

"Aye, and any person found giving help to the

English pirates will be fined and banished. So take care!" With a parting grin, he dodged the corncob Dirck sailed after him and left.

One hundred guilders! *By hemel*, old Pieter Minuit had paid the Wilden only sixty guilders for the whole island of the Manhattes! Feeling against the English must be running high, Dirck told himself. This was made clear to him that same day.

He took time to walk the length of the city wall. He saw that it was built like the usual stockade, with tree trunks fitted tightly together and their tops sharpened to a point. Along the inner side of the wall, a dirt walk had been built up for the soldiers to stand on.

The gates were closed at night. A burgher, or citizen, guard manned the one at Heere Street and also the guardhouse at the East River road entrance.

Dirck stopped to read the placard nailed on the wooden door of the Town Hall. It offered one hundred guilders reward for the capture of any Englishman who claimed to be a privateer under the flag and seal of the Rhode Island or Connecticut Plantations.

A few minutes later he listened to two fat burghers talking on their front door benches. They were dressed in gray jackets and baggy breeches, smoking

68

their long slender clay pipes in the warm April sun.

"*Ach hemel!*" said one of them. "I knew all along it was a mistake to let so many English settle in New Netherlands. There are four English villages on Long Island, as many as we ourselves have there. Don't tell me they aren't giving food and shelter to some of these English robbers. Even here in New Amsterdam there are enemies." The burgher puffed furiously on his pipe.

The other frowned under his high-crowned black hat. "And why did these English leave their New England plantations? Because they declare they have more freedom here. Now they use it against us."

"*Ach*, we don't have as much freedom here as we did back in Holland," the first burgher exclaimed. "All because of the West India Company's rules! Back home we chose our town schout, our schepens, and the two burgomasters." He raised his voice angrily. "While here our tyrant Stuyvesant picks them for us. Soon, but soon, this will change . . ."

"Hush, Johan!" The second man had noticed Dirck. "There stands the pirates' spy and his dog."

Dirck flushed, clenched his fists, then hurried on. What use to say anything?

So the townsfolk hated their Director-General's highhanded manners and wanted to rule themselves.

He couldn't blame them. Whatever freedom he'd had before the shipwreck was now lost to him.

Who was he? Let me know soon, oh Lord, he prayed.

The next evening, just as Long Mary lit the candles in their wooden holders, Sam Low pushed open the door to the kitchen lean-to.

He had been gone two days. His hair hung in black wisps under his old fur hat. His long brown jacket was streaked with soil.

Still wearing his hat, Sam Low sat down at the table with a scowl. He did not say the usual Dutch meal prayer. Instead, he broke off a hunk of bread, took the one knife that lay in the center of the worn, checked linen cloth, and smeared butter on the hunk. Long Mary ladled out the samp, a stew of cornmeal and meat, onto his wooden trencher.

Sam washed the food down with a mug of cider. Then he dropped his large horn spoon on the table.

Dirck felt the man's sharp eyes on him and stopped eating.

"After the bell rings tonight, I've an errand for you," Sam said.

After the bell rings! Dirck drew in his breath sharply. He knew that no one was to be on the streets after the bell rang at nine o'clock.

70

"The night watch, sir," he said, looking down at his trencher.

"Silence!" The trader slapped the table. "If your brains are as quick as your tongue, you'll have no trouble slipping past a night watch of stupid burghers." A sneer twisted his thin face.

"Yes, sir," Dirck replied. "But I do not know the streets at night."

"I'll give you directions. See that you heed them. What do you think I've kept you for? Now fetch me a sharp quill and my ink horn. I'll write a note for you to take to my friend," Sam said.

Dirck brought them to him. The trader went into his shop and closed the door. Dirck fed Lion and took him out into the back garden.

"Wait here for me, old fellow. You're going along tonight," he said with more brightness than he felt.

Lion thumped his tail as if he understood.

It was shortly after the nine o'clock bell when Dirck left the cottage. The back gate squeaked as he softly opened it. He followed a narrow path behind the bark mill, with Lion beside him. He could hear the old mill horse snuffling and stamping in the dark.

The two bulky packages he was carrying weighed

71

him down. He hoped he could find the taproom where he was to leave them.

"In the alley opening upon the Strand near the wall," Sam had told him in describing the place.

Dirck moved carefully through a night as black as Lion's fur. Coming out into a narrow lane, he stumbled over a chunk of wood. He gasped at the pain in his toe, then listened to make sure the night watch was not near.

A dog barked, and Lion growled in his thoat. Dirck dropped a bundle and put his hand over Lion's mouth to keep him from barking. They would go to jail if they were caught!

What was in his heavy bundles? They smelled like new-dried fur. He felt sure that trader Low had not paid the West India Company's tax, due on all furs to be exported to Europe. He was carrying smuggled furs!

Streaks of light came from the small windows of an inn. He caught a glimpse of two foreign sailors playing at "trock" on a game table inside. A gust of laughter followed him as he ran past.

He glanced over his shoulder and again stopped to listen a moment. Still no guard coming. Lion stood silently beside him.

"Good dog!" Dirck whispered.

Another corner and they came out into the Strand, the river road, which ran past the wall and out to the Long Island ferry. Dirck could hear the wash of the incoming tide on the wide shore.

"The narrow alley only two houses from the wall gate." Dirck repeated Sam Low's instructions. He knew that the wooden gate at the wall was closed against Wilden and strangers. Would a guard be there or making its rounds?

Just then he heard the voices of the night watch. He dropped down behind a wooden bench on a door stoop.

The voices faded away. The men were marching along the wall and away from the river. Dirck heaved a big sigh of relief and went on. His eyes had now grown used to the darkness. Dragging his bundles, he fumbled his way into a narrow alley.

Suddenly a candle flickered in the window of a dark hump of a house at the end of the blind alley. Then a second one shone.

That's the one, Dirck thought. He struggled up to the door, and knocked softly . . . one, one-two-three, one, one-two-three.

The top part of the divided door widened a crack.

"Master Low sent me," Dirck whispered. "With a package."

73

The door swung in enough to let Dirck wriggle through with his heavy burden. He stood facing a squat, ugly man only a little taller than himself. The tapster wore a red leather apron and a scowl.

Dirck held out a folded piece of brown paper. "Master Low wrote a message on this, which I'm to deliver here."

The tapster put his hand behind his back and shook his head. "'Tis not for me. I can't read. It's for *him*. And I'll have no more to do with *him* or this affair, I swear to that."

Dirck didn't know what to say. He put the note on the table nearest him. "What shall I do now?"

"Wait over there," the little man mumbled. He waved a long arm toward the high-backed settle standing out from one side of the fireplace. "I'll not be back."

With a sniff and a grumble, the tapster clumped up the rude stairsteps nailed against a side wall. He disappeared in the blackness above.

Dirck felt strange, alone in the dank, smelly room. He looked about at the long trestle table and benches, the wood tankards lined on a shelf, and the barrels in racks against one wall.

He did not wish to stand in the firelight. He dropped his bundles on the floor beside the settle.

74

Behind it he made out a sleeping bench built along the wall. He curled up there in a dark corner, his hand lying on Lion's head.

The creak of the unlatched door slowly opening awakened Dirck. A growl rumbled in Lion's throat and Dirck clasped his hand quickly about Lion's mouth. By the dim light of the candle he saw three men, in the knitted stocking caps and short canvas jackets of sailors, slip into the room. Right behind them came a taller, plume-hatted man in a plain doublet and sea boots.

After a swift glance around, the tall man went to the stairs and stood with his back to Dirck.

He doesn't see me yet, Dirck thought from behind the wood settle.

"You, up there. Where are Sam's bundles?" the man rasped out. The tapster refused to answer him.

Dirck grew stiff with shock. He had heard that raspy voice before. It was . . . it was . . . on shipboard!

The tall man turned around, and the firelight touched his face.

Dirck gasped aloud in horror. He'd seen the face that went with the voice before, too. That thin black mustache above a cruel mouth, he remembered . . . and the small, pointed beard, silver-streaked. But the black patch which covered one eye was new.

75

The man took a step forward, while his sailors guarded the door. A wary look came over his bony face. His hand covered one of the four pistols which hung from a red sash slung over his shoulder and tied at his other hip.

"Come out into the light," he hissed in English.

To Dirck's utter surprise, Lion stood up and growled. Then he walked to the center of the room, his broad head thrust forward, his lips curled back in a snarl. Yet he had obeyed the English commands of a strange man!

At the same moment Dirck saw the gleam of a silver pin fastened to the man's red sash. It was in the shape of a half-moon.

"Uncle Nicholas' silver half-moon!" Dirck cried out. And in that perilous instant he remembered everything.

CHAPTER SIX

The Pirates

DIRCK CROUCHED in the dark corner of the tap-room, a wave of memory washing over him. At last he knew!

He knew his name was Dirck de Weber of Rotter-dam. The man standing in the dim firelight, the pirate Thomas Baxter, had captured him on his way to the New World in the *Gilded Beaver* and had left him to die alone on Baxter's sloop when it sank in the terrible storm.

So Captain Baxter and his men had escaped from the sea, too! Baxter's eye must have been hurt. But what had happened to Uncle Nicholas, who had sailed with him on the *Gilded Beaver?* The silver half-moon was his. It was a prized family jewel.

And is Lion the pirate's dog, after all, he thought sadly.

77

All these things flashed through Dirck's head in the second before he saw Thomas Baxter give Lion a hard kick.

With a sharp yelp of pain, Lion turned and fastened his teeth into the pirate's thigh.

"Get this black imp loose," Baxter yelled. One of the sailors grabbed Lion and pulled him off. The next moment he was rolling on the floor with the snarling dog.

Dirck leaped forward from his dark corner with a cry. "Stop that! Let Lion be!"

Baxter whirled upon Dirck. "By the living thunder, you're alive!" he snarled in Dutch. "Seize him, swabbers."

Dirck had eyes only for the silver half-moon on Baxter's scarf. Wildly he rushed at the pirate captain and tore the pin loose. Baxter's arm struck his chest, knocking him against the stairs.

Another pirate burst into the room from his post outside. "Off with ye! The night watch is coming, captain. Out the back way."

"Bring the boy, Flips," Captain Baxter ordered a flat-nosed sailor, who wore a purple and red striped scarf tied around his knitted cap and a gold earring in one ear.

At once the ugly Flips seized Dirck and clamped

a hand over his mouth. In the struggle, the silver half-moon slipped from Dirck's fingers. Flips rushed him out the back way with drawn cutlass.

The pirates moved like shadows through the swampy field behind the taphouse. They circled south, then east toward the river road. They came out where Hoogh Street sloped down to meet the road near the wall. The vacant plot of land at this point was covered with bushes and trees, which made it a good hiding place. There was only the road between them and the empty river shore.

The men dropped silently to the ground among the bushes, just before the burgher watch hurried past. As he lay on the grass, Dirck's heart beat so fast he could hardly breathe.

What would the pirates do to him? Why did they even want him? Maybe because he was a witness to Sam Low's fur smuggling and his dealings with the English enemy?

Dirck did not dare cry out. If the watch found him with the pirates, the people would be certain that he was one of them. For even if the pirates feared him as a witness, Dirck guessed that the townspeople would not believe him. The best reason for his silence was Flip's cutlass against his back.

Lion had disappeared. Dirck hoped that he wasn't lying hurt and alone. Now he understood why the dog had been slow to obey his Dutch commands. Lion had understood only English!

"On your feet," Captain Baxter whispered.

Dirck was pulled to his feet and led across the river road to the sandy shore. One of the men found the jolly boat they had pulled up above the tide. After getting in, two of the pirates rowed them up the East River. They passed the little guardhouse on shore at the end of the city wall without trouble. All was quiet except for the dip of the oars.

They rowed on until they passed the dock and warehouse of old Isaac Allerton, the merchant. A darker shadow loomed ahead of them in the river. The pirate's ship! Dirck thought.

Should he jump overboard and try to swim to shore? A pistol shot would miss in the dark. Perhaps Captain Baxter would not fire and make a noise. Dirck clutched the boat's rough gunwale. Flips sat next to him with his cutlass ready.

Dirck heard a faint splashing in the distance. It sounded as if someone were swimming out from shore.

Just then a low groan rang out, and Baxter demanded, "Who has the furs?"

"Not me, cap'n."

"Not me, sir."

"Nor me." The men sounded half-afraid.

"By the living thunder!" Baxter hissed. "Did none of you pig's heads bring them?"

The pirate captain stood up and jerked Dirck's guard over to him. "Flips, you bilge rat, you were to look after them. Blast my scuppers, but you'll go back for 'em. Night watch or no!"

Dirck chose this moment to slip over the side of the boat. No one noticed him in their attention to the captain's rage.

Dirck dropped silently into the cold river. He swam under water until he thought his lungs would burst. When he finally came up for air, he heard a racket in the boat behind him.

81

The pirates had discovered he was gone. Their boat was turning in circles. He swam under water again.

Next time he rose for air, he heard Baxter shout, "Swim to shore after him, Flips!" Then came a splash as the pirate dived in.

Dirck felt a sharp fear. Even though he was a strong swimmer, the pirate might catch him. If he just had the strength to reach shore first, he might be able to hide in the darkness.

Behind him he heard Flips stroking through the water. Suddenly the man gave a muffled shout. "Help! Help!" he bubbled, as if he were being dragged under water.

Dirck could hear him thrashing about. "Stop him. Help . . . you men!"

The gasps of the pirate and yelps of a dog were a fearsome thing to hear in that wet, cold darkness.

Good old Lion! Dirck thought. He must have followed the boat along shore, then swum out to seek me. Now he's keeping Flips from catching up with me.

He felt gravel under his feet and dragged himself gratefully ashore. The struggle out in the water had ended. The pirates' boat was picking up Flips, Dirck decided, from the splashing he heard.

A dog barked back on the hill beyond the shore. Dirck stumbled along the water's edge, shivering in the spring air. He came to the log and plank supports of the Allerton dock. He crawled into the small sandy space under it and lay there, trying to get back his breath and strength.

The sound of the jolly boat's oars faded away. Was Baxter going back for his furs and to look for him later, at dawn?

I can't stay here, he told himself. But where's Lion?

He heard someone walk down to the dock. "Who goes there?" a man called out. Faint light came from a swinging horn lantern. The warehouse watchman, Dirck thought. Anyone finding me outside the wall might make trouble for me, for who would believe my story?

He lay still under the dock, afraid to make a sound. At last the man went away, and Dirck breathed easier.

Now he gave a low whistle. Once, twice. In a short while he felt a cold nose touch his neck. A wet Lion crawled in with him, whining for joy.

Dirck hugged him happily. "You don't know how glad I am you got away all right. You saved me again out there, Lion. Good dog, good dog," he said over and over, while Lion licked his face. "Just let anyone say you're Captain Baxter's dog now! You're mine."

Was there ever a smarter dog than Lion, he wondered.

But he couldn't stay here and freeze. He would have to get into the city again. Maybe Anneke or Hans would give him shelter. With the gate closed at night, the only way past the guardhouse would be by water.

I'll start running the half-mile back to town, he decided, and swim past the guardhouse.

He had taken only a few steps when he fell over a hard object. Under his hands he felt the bow of a small canoe pulled up on shore above the tide!

He could hardly believe his good luck. He walked around the canoe and found its square-bladed paddle stuck into the sand. Quickly he pushed on the bow with all his might. The canoe slid into the water, and he and Lion jumped into it. Then he grabbed the paddle and set to work.

He strained his eyes and ears through the darkness, wondering if the pirates' boat would appear beside him. When he came to the town wall and its guardhouse, he lay down in the canoe. The current carried it downriver, safely past the place.

At once he headed for the shore to beach the canoe. Then he caught his breath. A few feet from him he saw the dim outline of the pirates' jolly boat, lying empty. It must belong to the pirates, for no townsman would leave a boat lying here overnight. They had returned to the taphouse.

He must move fast. Again he pushed off and paddled on down until he reached the town dock. Just as he climbed onto it, he heard the call, "Twelve o'clock, and all's well."

"The burgher watch!" he whispered to Lion. "Coming down the Marckveldt Road from the fort."

Dancing light from its lanterns and torch reached ahead of the guard down the sloping road.

Dirck whirled about and jumped into the canoe. With quick strokes he sent it out into the river's flow.

A three-quarter moon poked its face through dark clouds. By its light Dirck saw a trading sloop anchored out in the stream. I'll stow aboard there until dawn, he thought, and then leave.

When he reached the sloop, he made fast the canoe's line to a rope ladder hanging from the side. He climbed aboard and pulled Lion up.

He saw the lights of the night watch moving along the Strand past Van der Grist's warehouse. Thank the stars, he had escaped unseen!

He lifted his head and listened. Heavy snores rolled from the other end of the sloop. Dirck moved forward as carefully as he could around the piles of boxes and barrels. He could barely see the black shape of a man lying on a cabin roof, wrapped in a blanket and sound asleep.

He crept back to where he felt a canvas covering some boxes. He lifted the cover, snapped his fingers for Lion, and crawled under it.

Everything was still. He could hear only the water lapping and the snores of the watchman.

He curled up against a bale and shivered in his wet clothes. I'll leave before the sailor wakes at dawn, he thought. It will be dangerous to go back to Sam Low's. And what about his note that I left at the taphouse. Was it about me?

How he wished he could be back in the old Netherlands instead of in this smelly place! How could he have imagined that the New World would be finer than home?

For the first time he had a chance to think about his family in Rotterdam. He saw them clearly . . . his father Joris de Webber, master weaver with his gentle face and stooped shoulders, his dear mother Hendrickie, little sister Marie, and small brother Pieter. He imagined they were smiling at him.

Surely Father was better after his slight heart attack, Dirck told himself. Because of this attack, Dirck remembered Father had not made his first trading voyage with Uncle Nicholas to the New World.

That was how the brave idea had come to Dirck, the idea of secretly taking his father's place aboard the *Gilded Beaver*, which was waiting in Rotterdam's river. Dirck wanted nothing more than to see the wonderful world across the ocean . . . to touch the peacocks under the palm trees on Hendrik Hudson's river, to find the gold that sparkled everywhere. Father's books and maps told all about it.

He had stowed aboard, leaving only a note behind to explain to his family.

Dirck sighed and clasped his knees tightly under the dark canvas. There were no peacocks, no earth glittering with gold here. Now he could recall, one by one, all the things that had happened to him just before the shipwreck.

First, there was the capture of the little yacht, *Gilded Beaver*, off Long Island Sound. Captain Thomas Baxter called himself an English privateer instead of a pirate. He flew the flag of Rhode Island. He spoke Dutch easily, having lived in New Amsterdam.

Next, the pirate captain had sent the *Gilded Beaver* to Rhode Island as a prize of war. Along with it went the crew and its few passengers.

Dirck and Uncle Nicholas would have gone there, too, if it hadn't been for the silver half-moon. That precious family medal had been a gift years ago from the explorer Hendrik Hudson. Captain Baxter had found it while searching Uncle Nicholas' clothes.

"Aha!" the pirate captain cried, holding the fine silver medal aloft.

"No, no," Dirck shouted wildly. He tried to snatch it back, fighting and kicking at Baxter's sea-boots.

A flat-nosed pirate had knocked him to the deck-boards, and Thomas Baxter, a black scowl on his face, ordered Dirck and Uncle Nick to be taken aboard his own sloop.

"This bold lad's to be used as a cabin boy, and both are to be sold as bondservants in Virginia," the pirate ordered in a fury.

And so, for the first time, they had lost the silver half-moon.

Dirck soon learned that the trading sloop they were on had been stolen from Hempstede, one of the English villages on Long Island, shortly before

the *Gilded Beaver* was captured. As he climbed aboard the sloop, he noticed that a board had been hastily nailed over the sloop's name.

A few hours later a sudden gale roared over the stolen ship. It swept wave after wave across the deck.

Dirck still could hear Baxter's voice shouting, "Abandon ship!" above the scream of the gale.

Ach, now he remembered something else! At the captain's cry, he had darted below to untie the black dog he'd seen there and petted. He could not let the animal drown.

Back on deck with the dog, Dirck saw the crew struggle to get into a small boat and cast off. Was that Uncle Nick at the rail, helping? Dirck could only cling with numb fingers to a line on the mast, while cold salt water swirled over him.

Through the spray and rain, he saw a wave wash a man at the rail into the sea. Then the small boat was gone.

"Uncle Nick!" Dirck cried out in terror, but the wind tossed his words away. Yes, that lost man could have been his uncle, and he was left alone on the doomed ship.

Then he heard the mainsail above his head snap loose. He felt the ship quiver as it split on the reef off Eaton's Neck. Down came the mast with a crash.

That was the last thing he remembered until he woke on the beach with Lion. Dirck put out his hand to touch the dog lying near him under the canvas.

He thought, I can tell General Stuyvesant my real name and story. I hope he will trust me and help me earn passage home. He can send a message back by the next ship and tell my family I'm safe, and about Uncle . . . Oh, poor Uncle Nicholas!

He choked back his sobs and dropped off into an uneasy sleep.

Someone stepped on his foot. Someone lifted back the piece of canvas and then pushed in beside him.

"Who? What?" Dirck was alert at once. Lion growled.

"Ssh!" a boy's voice said. "By Saint Nicholas, could it be Dirck?"

"Who . . . who is it?" Dirck, alarmed, tried to see the face in the light from a dawn-streaked sky.

The canvas dropped back over their heads, and in the dark Dirck felt a hand clutch his arm. "Don't be scared. It's Hans Kregier. What are you doing here?"

CHAPTER SEVEN

Stowaways

Huddled there under the sloop's canvas, Dirck could hardly believe his ears.

"Hans?" he whispered. "It can't be." He ran his fingers over the other's face.

"*Ja*, yes, it is," excitedly returned the boy. "What a surprise to find you here!"

"I'm hiding from someone. But you saw my canoe tied to the sloop? It's time for me to go ashore," Dirck told him.

"I saw one floating away," Hans said.

"Oh," groaned Dirck. "It came untied. What'll I do?"

"Just give me more room," Hans replied. "I'm looking for a place to stow away. This'll be fine. Whom are you hiding from, Dirck NoName?"

Dirck tried to wriggle over for Hans. "There,

92

how's that? Hans, I'm hiding from Thomas Baxter and his pirate crew. They tried to kidnap me tonight, but I escaped. Hans, I know that Sam Low is a traitor!"

"You're cracked in the head," Hans whispered back after a moment.

"I swear it's true. And the crack in my head is well, Hans. I remember my name and family perfectly. Isn't that wonderful? I'm Dirck de Webber of Rotterdam, and . . ." In as few words as possible, he told Hans about his night's adventures.

"*Hemel*, what a night!" his friend exclaimed. "I'm glad you escaped the pirates, and that your memory is back. Whatever will happen to you next? You're going to tell the Town Council everything, of course. How I wish I could stay here to see the excitement!" He sighed. "But I shall be far away this morning."

Dirck lifted the canvas for a bit of fresh air. "I've just got to go, now. Did you make fast your boat, Hans?"

"No! I let it go. Please stay longer with me, Dirck. This sloop is going upriver all the way to Fort Orange. From there I'm going to visit the Maquas. I plan to study the animals, plants, and customs of all the Wilden tribes in New Netherlands.

I'm going to draw them so people in other countries will know what they are really like." Hans sounded very serious.

Dirck was too surprised to speak at first. "Think of the danger!" he said, at last. "I didn't know you could draw. What about your father?"

"This is Father's sloop, the *Sea Mew*," Hans replied. "It's sailing this morning. You see, Father thinks wanting to be an artist is folly. So I'm going to show him. I'll make my own way."

"May you have better luck than I've had," Dirck said. "Your father doesn't know about this?"

"No. General Stuyvesant sent him north to New England on a mission to complain about the English pirates. I told our housekeeper I'm leaving. I know that Skipper Van Voort would never let me sail without Father's permission. That's why I'm stowing aboard."

"It's for you to decide, Hans. I promised Uncle Nick never to stow away again." Dirck was growing impatient to leave. "I can't stay longer; it's growing lighter." He lifted the canvas.

But at that moment he heard a boat bump against the side of the *Sea Mew* and a loud voice call out, "Ahoy there, Claes. Where are you, you lazy fellow?"

"The skipper!" He ducked back.

He heard a grumble and a groan. Then Claes, the mate, came staggering along the deck.

"What shall I do now?" Dirck whispered in Hans's ear. "If your skipper sees me, he'll beat me."

"Stay here for a while," Hans pleaded. "If you go out, Skipper Van Voort will find me, too, and make me go home. Please, Dirck. You can slip away while they finish loading. Go later, when he isn't watching."

Dirck hesitated. He could hear the skipper scolding the mate for sleeping late and Claes's mumbled answers. There were more rumbles and thumps as dock porters dropped a load near the boys' hiding place.

"All is ready, mate. That's the last of it," the skipper shouted. "Hoist the anchor. Let fly the mains'l. Ho, what's wrong with you, Claes?"

Dirck stiffened. Only one load! Most of the cargo was aboard when he came, then. Now what was he going to do?

"Hans," he pleaded. He felt the boat move slowly, then faster as a light breeze caught her sail.

"Ssh!" Hans said, for the skipper stamped by.

Dirck listened in a daze to the skipper's crisp orders. He did not want to go to Fort Orange far

95

up the Hudson. He wanted to go back to Holland and his family.

The sloop rounded the Capske rocks at the tip of the island and entered Hudson's vast river. Five minutes passed, then fifteen. Dirck grew more tense with each passing minute. He would not be able to stand it much longer. They must be past the town. He'd have to make a dash for it and jump overboard.

Van Voort was passing their hiding place again. Lion chose this very moment to give a loud yawn that was half whine, "Aw-aw-awhr-rr." He was growing tired of their cramped quarters.

The skipper's footsteps stopped. "What's that?" he cried.

Dirck froze. To his surprise he heard the skipper say, "Claes! Are you making sport of me back there by yawning behind my back?"

Dirck couldn't hear the answer, but he felt Hans's shoulders shaking with laughter. He covered his mouth with his hand to silence his own chuckles.

Lion yawned loudly again. "Aw-awh-r-r-r."

"Claes! Do you dare to make fun of me?" the skipper roared. Then, "You say you didn't make the noise? Who did? What's wrong? You look strange, man."

Claes replied, "I'm very ill, skipper."

There was a silence, and suddenly the canvas covering the boys was thrown aside. They blinked up at the skipper, a huge man with a reddish-blond beard. He caught an arm of each boy and lifted him to his feet with one swift movement.

"So here are the little noisemakers, *ja?*" he demanded, shaking them. "Who said you could hide aboard my ship? With a dog, too! What trick is this?"

"Please, Skipper Van Voort," Hans managed to gasp out. "It's I, Hans Kregier. I want to sail with you."

The skipper dropped Hans's arm and peered into his face. "Thunder and lightning! It's the master's boy!"

"Of course." Hans calmly pulled down his brown jacket and put his arm about Dirck's shoulders. "Dirck, here, is my good friend. I want him to come with us," he told the amazed skipper.

"I can't take you without your father's permission," the sloop captain stormed.

"Well, sir . . ." Dirck spoke up in spite of the odd feeling in the pit of his stomach. "I don't want to stay aboard. I have to get back to town. Will you please put Lion and me ashore right now? We are close enough to it."

"You ask me to turn my *Sea Mew* about and take you back to town or to shore? No!" roared Van Voort. He pounded his freckled fist into his other hand.

Hans smiled a little. "Then we'll have to stay aboard, sir. You say yourself that . . ."

"I'll toss you overboard," the skipper threatened, but he looked less angry.

"Over there, sir," Dirck suddenly pointed. "Your mate has fallen."

The skipper whirled about. The mate had fallen with a groan over the steering tiller.

The skipper rushed to him. Claes's face was a feverish red, and his eyes were closed.

"You, boy, help me carry him to his bunk," Van Voort ordered. "Hans, take the tiller." The sloop was yawing.

"Ay, ay, sir," Hans answered readily. Then Dirck and the skipper, followed by Lion, carried the sick man into the tiny cabin. They placed him gently on a straw mattress.

"How can I manage alone?" the skipper groaned. "Claes needs care, too, poor fellow. I hope it isn't the pox."

The pox! Dirck shivered at that dreadful word.

Van Voort must have seen the swift fear in Dirck's

98

eyes. "But there's no pox about," he went on quickly. He handed Dirck a gourd of water. "Put a wet rag on his face and cool it. Then watch him from outside the cabin door. Hans can help me." He stopped, and then he growled, "You'll both have to stay aboard now, Lord help me! The sloop's lost way, and those black clouds spell rain."

He started to go up the few steps from the cabin. Lion, too, decided to go and crowded against the skipper's legs to get there first. Van Voort lost his footing, falling flat on his face in the doorway.

He crawled out on deck, then turned and shook his fist at Lion. "Thunder and lightning!" he bellowed, while he rubbed his shin. "Get that Wilden dog out of here. Twice I've stumbled over him. Off he goes and right now! Up on deck and hurry!"

Dirck gave the purple-faced skipper a pleading look. "Oh no, please. He didn't mean any harm."

Van Voort got to his feet and made for the tiller. "Off he goes," he shouted over his shoulder.

Dirck went outside and found Lion hiding behind a barrel. He saw that the *Sea Mew* was going inshore as close as she could safely go. Van Voort gave the tiller back to Hans and set one of the leeboards into the water.

"Come here, you two," he called to Dirck.

99

Dirck went forward slowly, his hand on Lion's broad head. "Skipper Van Voort," he began, and his voice shook. "Lion and I are sorry about your fall. But we'll be careful." The words came in a rush, now. "I promise to keep Lion out of your way. Please let me keep him. I'm all he's got."

The captain scowled. "I've no time to listen to your troubles. Haven't I enough trouble with a sick mate and two wooden-head boys, besides a storm threatening? I don't want the dog aboard. Cast him off. He can swim ashore and make his way back to town."

Dirck looked at the rocky, tree-covered shoreline. He set his jaw, and his face burned. "No, I can't do that. He might starve."

"*Ach*, he can hunt for himself. Don't tempt me, boy, or I might toss you in, too."

With that, the skipper picked up Lion and threw him into the river.

Dirck's cry was drowned in the great splash as Lion hit the water. Dirck lunged forward, then felt Van Voort holding him back. In a few seconds he saw Lion bob up and begin to swim strongly.

The dog made straight for the sloop. But the skipper, back at the tiller luffed into the wind, and the ship ran upshore ahead of Lion.

100

Dirck and Hans watched anxiously, leaning over the side of the *Sea Mew*. At last they saw the dog, a black dot on the waves, strike out for shore.

Dirck's tense shoulders relaxed when Lion scrambled up the rocky bank. All Dirck could hope for now was that his dog could make his way back to New Amsterdam.

His throat was tight with sobs. What would he do without Lion? He had lost his best friend.

"I'll never see him again," he told Hans sadly.

CHAPTER EIGHT

Dirck's Story

THE RAIN BEGAN soon after Lion was tossed over-board.

It pelted down on the skipper at the tiller, and the boys sitting by the cabin door. They huddled together under a piece of tarred canvas, while the *Sea Mew* rolled and, inside, the delirious mate moaned.

Dirck felt miserable. He wondered where Lion was now. He hoped he would follow the shore downstream to town.

"How could the skipper do that?" he muttered angrily to Hans. "I'd beat him if I were big enough."

"He's worried," Hans said. "The river's rough, you know. Maybe we'll find Lion again when we return."

Dirck buried his head in his arms. So much had

102

happened to him since yesterday that it was hard to think straight. All that he remembered about his family and his sea voyage was burning inside him. He still couldn't tell the General or the Town Council so they could help him get home again.

Who knew? He might never come back from this trip into the wilderness.

After the rain and the rough waters, the gray clouds parted. The sun shone out. They had reached the Highlands, Hans told Dirck, as they looked up at the high rocks, topped by trees in spring green. The wind died away. Both mainsail and jib hung limp, and the little sloop barely moved.

"Break out the anchor—the tide's changing. We'll stop here for the night," the skipper decided. Hans and Dirck helped with the sails. Then the skipper went into the cabin and brought out cheese, milk and cider in stone jars, and the crumbly bread made from the Indian maize.

"*Ja.*" Skipper Van Voort almost smiled. "It is good, the cheese and milk from our fat Dutch cows."

"We had a cow named Spotty, once," Dirck remembered. He blinked rapidly.

Hans stared at him, while the leather-faced skipper went on chewing. "Do you know you haven't told me how you came to New Netherlands, Dirck?"

Dirck shrugged. "Who cares?" he mumbled. "No one in this wild land likes me."

Hans gave him a poke and laughed. "St. Nicholas! I like you and others in our town will, too. Have patience, wooden-head."

Dirck looked up. He saw the warm glow of friendship in Hans's eyes and felt better.

"All right, I'll tell you." He took a deep breath and began. "I wanted to come to the New World more than anything. I believed the tales written in Father's old books about it. Besides, I didn't like the Latin School I went to. I just like to swim and to skate on the canal in winter, and always have a good time. Maybe I was a little lazy."

He gave Hans a sheepish grin, for it was true.

"We skate and slide down the hills in winter, too," Hans replied. "But how did you sail here. And tell me more about the pirates, and how you were ship-wrecked."

"First things come first, as Long Mary says," Dirck replied. "My father and his older brother Nicholas are partners in a small weaving business. Uncle Nick isn't married, but even so they found it hard to make a living with so many other weavers in the Guild. So they planned a trading trip here to New Netherlands."

His mouth felt dry, and he took a sip of milk.

"Yes, yes, go on," Hans said impatiently.

"Well, they planned to sail on a ship carrying supplies to the patroon at Rensselaerswyck near Fort Orange. While here they intended to see if they could also set up a small weaving trade," Dirck said.

Skipper Van Voort stirred himself. "Our Dutch women don't take to spinning and weaving as well as the English women," he said.

Hans nodded. "Go on, Dirck." He got up, found a ship's horn lantern, and lighted it against the coming dusk.

Dirck changed his position on the coil of rope where he was sitting. "This sea war with England changed their plans. The yacht, *Gilded Beaver*, waited months in Rotterdam's river to sail. Then its skipper decided to join a New World convoy.

"But Father became ill with his heart just before sailing time. Uncle Nick had to go alone." Dirck stopped and sighed. "Only he didn't go alone. I stowed aboard the *Gilded Beaver* until we were out to sea. *Hemel*, he was angry with me!"

"Should have had your breeches warmed," growled the skipper.

Dirck knew that Van Voort was thinking about him and Hans. He said quickly, "He did that, sir.

I promised never to stow away again. Er . . . this time was an accident, skipper." He gave a sheepish grin.

He went on. "We weathered two storms. The second one blew us off course and away from the other ships, which were going to Virginia and the West Indies, anyway. So that's how we happened to come into the Sound, north of Long Island, instead of going south to New Amsterdam through the lower bay."

"Long Island Sound's where the pirates lie in wait," Hans put in eagerly.

Dirck nodded. "Suddenly a fast sloop bore down on us and before we knew it, they shot a cannon ball across our bow. Our skipper hove to, and the next thing Captain Baxter and his men were aboard us!"

Hans's face looked tense. "Did you fight them?"

"No, Hans. We had a small crew and Baxter a large one of fighting sailors. Baxter sent our yacht to Rhode Island as a prize of war. All the passengers went with it as prisoners, except Uncle Nick and me." He told them all about the pirate's taking the silver half-moon.

"What a story!" Hans said in an awed tone, trying to take it all in. "Then it really wasn't the *Gilded Beaver* that sank in the storm."

106

"No," Dirck said. He explained about the English trading sloop being stolen from Hempstede harbor, and how he had found Lion on it. "Whom Lion belongs to, or how he got there is more than I know. The storm soon hit us and drove us on to the reef near Oyster Bay." Dirck gulped. Then he said, "I'm sure Lion saved my life by swimming to shore with me." It was hard to talk about it all.

"Saint Nicholas!" Hans said with feeling. "I'm sorry for you and your uncle. Don't you really know what happened to him?"

Dirck shrugged his shoulders, and for a moment he couldn't speak. Then he described those last minutes in the storm.

When he had finished, Hans tried to comfort him. "Maybe your uncle got off in the pirates' jolly boat."

"No, I believe not," Dirck said. He sat quietly, thinking. He raised his head. "There's one thing I'm going to do. I'm going to get our silver half-moon back from that pirate Thomas Baxter if it takes me years."

"What does it look like?" The skipper finally spoke up, since he had finished his meal.

"It's a medal in the shape of a half-moon and has a clasp in the back. The name 'De Halve Maen' is written on its face. Forty-five years ago Hendrik

107

Hudson gave it to my great-uncle. He in turn left it to Uncle Nick, and I'm to have it next."

"It means a lot to you, of course," Hans said.

Dirck nodded. "You see, my great-uncle was mate on Hudson's yacht, *The Half Moon*, and so was one of the first white men to see this river in 1609. Every man on that voyage of discovery received a silver half-moon from Hudson," he said. "Truly, it was one of the reasons I wanted to come to the New World."

"*Ja*, I've heard that story," said the skipper, wiping his mouth with the back of his hand. "I can believe that part."

"Every word I've said is true," Dirck replied heatedly. "Our family name is cut into the back of the medal. It could be proof of who I was for your mean Sheriff Van Ten. If only I hadn't lost it again in that taphouse last night when I took the beavers to Thomas Baxter!"

"Taphouse? Beaverskins?" Van Voort suddenly straightened up.

Dirck could have bitten his tongue off. He didn't want to tell the skipper more, but Van Voort demanded to know.

After Dirck had explained as best he could, the skipper cried, "Thunder and lightning! You'll get

108

into a pack of trouble for your part in last night's business."

"But I didn't . . ." Dirck started to say.

Van Voort did not listen. "I'd say that Sam Low was trying to send those skins out of town without paying the export tax on them. Lord knows where he found them. Cheated the Wilden, no doubt. That's why they don't trust us honest traders. And you helped him trade with the enemy!" He snorted in disgust. "Do you know more about this than you're telling?"

"No, and Sam Low made me do it," Dirck said angrily.

Hans clapped his arm about Dirck's shoulders and said quietly, "Don't mind him, I believe you. You were lucky to give Baxter's pirates the slip. They are bad men. When we return I'll tell Father your story. He'll believe you, too. He's a . . . a fair man." Hans stammered over the last words.

Dirck gave him a quick look. "But if you go off into the land of the Maquas," he said, "how can you return with me?"

"Hm-m-m," the skipper was saying, while he looked at Dirck with a cold eye. "Maybe you have thrown in your lot with the pirates. Who knows? Maybe your Lion *is* the pirate's dog."

Dirck jumped to his feet. He had to leave before he shot out more angry words.

"I'll look in on Claes before I go to sleep," he said, making his way past the boxes and barrels to the tiny cabin.

At dawn the jerk of the sail's yardarm awoke Dirck. A light southeast breeze had sprung up. Dirck rolled out of his blanket and stretched stiffly.

He glanced in at the snoring Claes. His face was covered with a fine red rash.

"The pox!" Dirck gasped. He looked up and saw that the skipper and Hans were setting the sails, which grew fat in the breeze.

"Your mate's broken out with a rash," he shouted. "Come see, skipper."

Hans dropped a line and took the tiller. The skipper came hurrying. He gave a short laugh and wiped his red forehead when he saw Claes.

"This is not the pox," he declared. " 'Tis another sort of rash . . . the kind the young ones catch." He looked up and gave Dirck his first smile.

Dirck's heart dropped back into his chest. He was glad he need not fear the dread smallpox.

"We are lucky," he said simply. Things weren't so bad, after all. He skipped up the steps, whistling, to tell Hans that Claes did not have the pox.

110

The sloop sailed slowly up the river against a strong tide. Hans said the tides went up as far as Fort Orange. There was little traffic on the great river. Dirck saw a few Wilden log canoes close to the western shore. Once a trading yawl passed, going downstream with the swift current in the middle of the river. They hailed it but didn't stop.

They passed a small landing place where a few fields were being farmed.

By noon clouds covered the sun. Another shower blew up and the *Sea Mew* anchored in a small bay. When the rain ended, the sails flapped idly.

Dirck and Hans dived into the cold river for a brisk swim. Afterward, they fished and caught a striped bass as large as a codfish, and a big salmon.

They broiled them over a fire built on the square of stone and clay set out in the bow.

"Best fish I've ever eaten," Dirck said, after he bit into the crackling flesh. "Largest fish I've ever seen have been here in New Netherlands."

"Everything in the New World comes larger and finer than in the Old," Hans said loyally. "I am going to show that by my sketches."

He drew a picture of Dirck with a piece of charcoal on the brown canvas sail. Then he drew Lion with quick strokes.

111

Dirck stared at Lion's head. Had Hans heard what he had during the night, he wondered? He could have sworn that he heard Lion barking. But how was that possible? Probably it was wolves.

A ghostly fog drifted over the river with the dusk. It was not until the sun was high the next morning that the fog cleared. The tide changed and a south breeze blew.

By this time Claes began to feel a little better. "It was kind of you to care for me when I was so sick," he thanked Dirck weakly. "And me a stranger."

Dirck's face grew warm at the mate's praise. "Skipper's orders. I did my duty."

He smiled to himself at his words. At home in Rotterdam he had never bothered much about his "duty." Now thoughts of Mother and Father and his small brother and sister often filled his mind.

They didn't know yet about Uncle Nick and his bad fortune. How he wished he could tell them he was all right, and that he was sorry he left with only a good-by note, sorry he had been so thoughtless.

Every day he was moving farther away from New Amsterdam and from home. Would he ever see his family again?

As soon as the fog lifted, he helped make ready for the sail on up the river. "We've lost a day already," the skipper snapped.

But Dirck lifted his head. "Is that a dog barking?" he yelled excitedly.

CHAPTER NINE

North to the Maquas

DIRCK, HANS and the skipper all stopped work on the *Sea Mew*, holding the heavy lines in their hands. They listened.

Dirck's eyes searched the rounding shoreline below them. A moment before he thought he saw a black shadow move along a bare spot of Wilden maizeland. Then it disappeared into the fir trees. Perhaps it was a bear?

Now the animal broke out onto the bay shore. It stood barking at the sloop. Dirck answered with a wild shout, "It's Lion . . . Lion! He followed us all this way!"

Lion gave a sharp yelp and plunged into the water. He swam toward the *Sea Mew* with smooth powerful strokes.

Dirck jumped up and down with joy. "Lion,

come on! Skipper, Hans . . . Lion has followed us all the way along the shore."

"Thunder and lightning," muttered Van Voort and his mouth fell open in disbelief.

"What a dog! Keep coming, Lion," Hans shouted over the narrowing space of water.

Now the dog was close to the sloop's side. Dirck ripped off his shirt and breeches, and jumped overboard. He caught Lion in his arms and pushed him against the side so that Hans could reach down and grasp him. Then Dirck climbed quickly up the rope ladder.

He rolled the tired dog in a blanket Hans brought, in spite of Lion's wildly thumping tail. Then he dried himself with shaking hands.

He begged the watching skipper to allow Lion to stay aboard this time. "Please let him stay. He has run for days, has come so far. You can't turn him away now. He's a smart dog, and I'll keep him out of your way. I promise. Oh, please."

Dirck was beginning the same speech all over again, when the big skipper threw up his arms. "Stop, boy, stop! Take a breath and give me a chance to say something."

Dirck held his breath and stood very still over Lion. His dog looked up at him with glowing eyes and whimpered. Dirck patted his smooth head and waited for the skipper to speak.

"Thunder and lightning! You've talked me into it. Never knew a dog to do this before," Van Voort said, scratching his beard. "Suppose he's earned his right to come with us. But keep him from underfoot. Hans, up anchor and we'll get underway." Then he sat down and shoved over the tiller, only shrugging at the boys' happy thanks.

The *Sea Mew* turned easily. With a fresh breeze behind her, she sailed on north up the narrowing river.

The sun shone stronger, and Lion dozed with its warmth on his back. Dirck hung over him. Already he had given the dog cold fish and a ham bone to gnaw.

He still could not understand how Lion had found them. Except for worn paws and a few scratches, he seemed to be all right. He must have followed them along the shore even when they were out of sight. Thank Heaven, the weather had kept them from going too fast!

Oh, he and Lion would never part again! But what if Lion's former master should one day be found? Dirck couldn't bear the thought of it. He pushed that fear back into a corner of his mind.

116

During the days they sailed north, he was constantly amazed at the land's wild beauty. The rugged cliffs and hills crowned with forest on either side seemed as grand as any Old World church.

Great flocks of wild fowl lighted on the mighty waters, and large fish jumped happily in the moonlit ripples. Through rocky clefts deer came to drink and swim in the back pools of the river.

The skipper would bring out an old snaphance fowling piece just before dusk. He would load it with lead and fine powder. He easily brought down a dozen waterfowl with a shot or two.

Dirck almost hated to see the birds fall, but he knew they needed them for food. The first time the skipper shot, Lion at once jumped into the river and began to bring back the birds in his mouth. The boys got into the small boat tied on behind to help. When they were back on board Lion gave a mighty shake, wetting the skipper.

Van Voort opened his mouth, then snapped it shut, to Dirck's relief.

"Lion's working for us already," Hans reminded the skipper cheerily as he started to build a small charcoal fire on the clay hearth.

Since Claes's fever had now left him, the boys began to share the bunk opposite him. Van Voort took the first watch outside. Before they went to sleep, the boys would talk together in whispers. Dirck learned a few things about the Maquas from Hans in their talks.

"The Maquas' totem and their clan is that of the Bear. They call themselves 'People of the Bear.' Then there is a Tortoise and a Wolf clan, too," Hans said.

"One of the sachems in the first Maquas castle west of the fort traded with Father last summer when I came up," Hans went on. "His nephew, Young Bear, lives with him as his son. Young Bear will be a warrior next year when he's fourteen. He and I fished and swam together for three days."

"Did you learn to speak with him?" Dirck asked curiously.

"We could understand each other well enough with signs. I'll show you some of them tomorrow. Dirck—" Hans half sat up, leaning on one elbow— "I'm sure that if I followed the Wilden trail west to their village, or castle, I could live with them a while."

"What would you do there, Hans?"

"Many things," Hans said dreamily. "I'd learn the differences between their ways and those of the Hudson River tribes. I'd sketch them trapping and skin-

118

ning beaver. I'd watch them build their elm bark canoes, their Long Houses, and prepare and smoke their food."

"Has no one done this before?" Dirck was thinking about the dangers of such a trip.

"Yes, a friend of Father's by the name of Adriaen Van der Donck a few years ago. He has gone back to Holland to complain to the government about General Stuyvesant's rule. The General chooses New Amsterdam's schepens and burgomasters himself, instead of letting the people elect them as they do in Holland. Father says Mynheer Van der Donck wrote a book describing New Netherlands and printed it back in Holland. But I'll have sketches of the Maquas and River Indians and their villages to show in mine."

"Aren't the Maquas very fierce?" Dirck said. "Worse than the River Indians?"

"Yes, they're cruel to their enemies. They have fought and beaten the river tribes, and also the tribes near the English, the Mahikanders. The English call them Mohikans," Hans told him. "The Maquas couldn't have done this without the guns we traded them."

"But I thought that in New Amsterdam the people couldn't trade guns for beavers," Dirck interrupted.

"It's against the law."

"Well, they do so up in Fort Orange," Hans declared. "Since the English will not give the Mohikans guns, only the Maquas have them. That's why the Maquas are friendly to us Dutch, and I am not afraid to visit them. By Saint Nicholas, if it weren't for the Maquas, the River Indians would try to kill all of us!"

Dirck gulped and sat straight up in the dark. "Thunder and lightning!"

Hans chuckled. Then he continued, "Have you never heard of the war we had with the Wilden tribes around Manhattes ten years ago? I was a small lad, yet I remember how everyone gathered in the fort, while the nearby tribes burned our farms and killed many. At that time we had a wicked Director-General by the name of Van Kieft. He burned several Wilden villages, and that's why no tribes live close to New Amsterdam now."

"I . . . I didn't know." Dirck licked dry lips in the darkness, ready to hear shrill Wilden yells at any moment.

"We've had peace since the West India Company sent out Pieter Stuyvesant seven years ago to rule us," Hans consoled him. "Our colony has begun to grow again. Never as fast as the English colonies,

120

by hemel." He sighed. "I'd hate to see them swallow up our fine land."

"More Hollanders ought to come across the ocean, then," Dirck said sleepily. "I wonder if Father . . . if Father . . ." His eyes closed, and he slept soundly until his turn to take the watch.

The next morning they stopped at the tiny settlement at Esopus Creek on the river's west bank. Here they dropped off supplies and stretched their legs. All Dirck could see was a log trading house beside the creek, and a few farms encircled by the thick, dark forest.

"There's not even a stockade built here," Dirck remarked to Hans on their way back to the sloop.

Skipper Van Voort shook his head over this. "These folk are blockheads not to have a blockhouse," he snorted. "The river tribe here at Esopus, or Atkarkarton, doesn't welcome farmers on its corn land. Even if the tribe did sell it to them, there's bound to be trouble."

Dirck was glad he didn't live here. "Will there be trouble at Fort Orange, too?" he asked thoughtfully.

"No, not as long as we trade the Maquas guns and gunpowder for furs," Van Voort muttered. "But they might fight their enemies, the Mahikanders, who live east of this river . . ."

"I thought New Netherlands was short of gunpowder," Dirck began, and then stopped short. Anneke had said that, and then told him it was to be kept a secret.

Van Voort's seamed face grew hard as stone. "You and Hans get busy and cast off," he snapped. "No more questions."

Now the river became more difficult to sail. There were shoals and passages with the danger of running aground. The wind turned against them, so the *Sea Mew* anchored at Norman's Kill. Dirck saw two beautiful green waterfalls tumbling down into the river.

A light south breeze sent them slowly on the next day. The riverbanks grew flat with rolling hills behind them. They passed Beeren Island, where Dirck saw Wilden fishing with nets along the low banks of the smooth-flowing river.

Hans carefully packed away some charcoal sketches he had finished of the Esopus Creek settlement. He looked up at Dirck who had been playing with Lion. "We will soon be there, Dirck. I've been thinking . . . it might be best for us to call on Jan Baptiste van Rensselaer. He's Father's friend and

122

might offer us a bed. Unless you'd rather stay with the skipper and Claes?"

"No!" Dirck said sharply. Somehow he felt it would not be wise to be alone with Van Voort. "I wish I didn't have to sail back with him. And who is Jan Baptiste?"

"He's the director in charge of the great patroonship of Rensselaerswyck. His land stretches for twenty-four miles on both sides of the river, from Beeren Island there up to the mouth of the Maquas river. Jan Baptiste is one of the sons of the dead patroon, Kilaen Van Rensselaer, who was a diamond merchant in Amsterdam and . . ."

"Yes, I know," Dirck put in eagerly. "I heard Father speak of that Kilaen. He got large grants of land from the government and built up the only successful patroonship in New Netherlands, although he never came here. He sent farmers and their families over to help work the land, instead of just trading with the Wilden."

The *Sea Mew* skirted a small island. It passed a field of winter wheat, which showed green on the narrow plain along the crowding hills. Several men followed oxen, making the land ready for their oats and barley. Cow bells tinkled from a river meadow.

The *Sea Mew* rounded a bend and the first

thatched houses came into view on the west bank. A farmhouse or two showed on the east bank.

"Fort Orange!" Hans cried. "Or rather, Beverwyck. That's the new name General Stuyvesant gave the village. He and Jan Baptiste had a fight about it. Jan said the village belonged to the patroon and not to the West India Company. The General won . . . with a squad of soldiers."

The skipper's bellow made the boys jump. They hurried to obey his orders and anchor the *Sea Mew*. As they worked, Dirck cast a glance at the dark knot of villagers gathering in front of the fort.

Little Fort Orange sat close to the riverbank. The West India Company's trading house and a few cottages were inside its long stockade, Hans told him. Some forty houses were scattered around the fort and strung along the riverbank. A few were brick from the new brick works, but most were made of planks with thatched roofs.

Dirck took his eyes from the shore to catch the skipper's glance. The way Van Voort looked at him gave Dirck an uneasy feeling. Was something wrong?

The short, wiry Claes sat on a coil of rope and gave the boys a steady flow of advice. "Ye'll make good sailors yet," he told them. The mate seemed in a

124

happy mood, now that his strength was returning and his rash had faded.

Leaving Claes behind, the skipper and boys set out in the small rowboat for shore. Van Voort wished to arrange for a scow to come out and unload.

They drew near a short log pier, where Dirck saw a man in dark homespun waiting. He carried a ledger and was a clerk, no doubt. Behind him Dirck caught a glimpse of a Dutch soldier, a sergeant in helmet and breastplate over a leather jerkin. Farmers and traders in leather clothes and fur hats, children in blue aprons, and a few women made up the rest of the eager group.

Dirck was excited, too. He stood up, ready to jump onto the little pier.

He felt the skipper's thick fingers grip his arm tightly. "Stop, boy!" Van Voort ordered. He called over to the waiting clerk. "Is General Stuyvesant still there at the fort? I have a possible spy for him!"

Dirck couldn't believe his ears. Van Voort wanted to turn him in as a spy! The skipper hadn't believed his story!

"No! No!" he shouted.

With a quick lunge he wrenched himself free from the skipper, who was listening to the clerk's answer. He dived headlong into the river. He came up gasping and struck out blindly, the cries of the watchers in his ears.

Another splash! He looked over his shoulder as a current caught him. Lion's black head was moving his way through the water. Briefly he saw Hans and the skipper struggling in the boat for the oars. Some men were jumping into another small boat to give chase.

The tide was carrying Dirck past the landing place. Suddenly he saw a small bark canoe shoot out from shore. A Wild boy was guiding the canoe with swift motions of his square-bladed paddle.

What shall I do? Dirck thought desperately. I can't swim forever. It's better to let the savage pick me up than the skipper.

The Wild boy spoke guttural words as he helped Dirck into the flimsy canoe.

"Thank you," Dirck gasped after a moment. He clung shivering to the rough frame while the slender boy drove the canoe forward and parallel to the shore.

He stared at the boy's leather leggings that were held at the waist with a belt of seewan. A copper ornament decorated the bristly cockscomb of hair atop his shaven head. Did this handsome youth understand any Dutch, Dirck wondered?

126

"Maquas?" he asked, after a quick glance told him that the villagers' boat had turned back. Even Lion was swimming back to shore.

"What's your name and where are we going?" Dirck said again.

The Wild's black eyes glittered. He touched his bare chest on which hung strings of bear's teeth and beads of seewan. "Young Bear," he said.

"Thanks, Young Bear." Dirck tried to give him a friendly smile through his blue lips. "You saved my life. I thought I might drown." He struck his own chest. "I'm Dirck."

Soon he heard Lion bark and looked toward the high riverbank. He caught glimpses of the dog running through the bushes and trees as he followed the canoe's progress.

Young Bear now guided it into another landing place. Dirck guessed that this was about a mile north of the village.

He saw a stockade, and within it a three-story stone and wood house with a thatched roof. It was built into a hilly slope. A flag waved at the top of a flagpole and a path led down to the landing place.

Young Bear pointed to a young man of medium height, who was striding down the path. "Sachem . . . big chief," he said.

127

Dirck stepped out of the canoe slowly as Young Bear beached it beside the few logs that made a dock. The young man came on to meet them. He wore a determined look on his round face with its tiny black mustache, and tiny pointed beard.

Dirck felt his scalp prickle, and he clenched his fists. Was this "big chief" going to jail him, too? Had he jumped from the frying pan into the fire?

CHAPTER TEN

A Fish Caught at Night

DIRCK BRACED HIMSELF to face this important stranger. He could see that the young man had a special air about him. It was in the way he held his head, his dark hair touching the "falling collar" on his silver-buttoned jacket. Dirck could see it in the way the man stood, his sturdy legs in stockings of English silk. His leather shoes were even tied with fashionable ribbon bows.

The man wasted no time in saying, "Whom do you bring to me, Young Bear?" His glance, under his wide hat, moved swiftly from water-soaked Dirck to Young Bear's face.

The Wild lad stood straight as a pine tree and said nothing.

Dirck raised his chin and met the man's eyes. "Young Bear pulled me from the river," he said.

"My name is Dirck de Webber. My father is a master woolworker in Rotterdam."

"Rotterdam, eh? And what do you here?" the young man asked mildly.

"Mynheer, I sailed to New Amsterdam with my uncle, who was lost at sea. We were captured by English pirates but I escaped. Then I came upriver on the *Sea Mew* with Hans Kregier. Skipper Van Voort thought I was a spy for the pirates or the English. He tried to turn me over to General Stuyvesant at Fort Orange. I'm no spy, mynheer. I don't want to go to jail, either."

"So? *Hemel*, what a story! I am Jan Baptiste Van Rensselaer, director of the colony of Rensselaerswyck." The young man put his hands behind his back and swayed a little where he stood, thinking. "But what am I to do with you? The Honorable General Stuyvesant left Fort Orange several days ago. You must have passed him on the river. He ought to be back in his hornet's nest by this time." He winked slyly.

Dirck began to feel better. At the same moment he heard a deep "Woof, woof!" Lion dashed out of the pine grove and on down to the bank, his pink tongue bright against his black muzzle.

With a happy yelp he almost knocked Dirck over

in his delight at finding him again. Next, he whirled about and excitedly jumped on Jan Baptiste.

"Stop, Lion! No, no!" Dirck cried. "Down!" He stared in dismay at the muddy streaks on Van Rensselaer's wide breeches. "Lion!" he scolded weakly, pushing him aside.

Redfaced, he bent to brush off the mud. "I'm sorry, mynheer. Lion doesn't understand Dutch well."

Jan Baptiste wiped Lion's wet kiss from his face. He began to shake. He was laughing! And so Dirck laughed, too, for the first time that day.

Also, for the first time, he noticed that several yellow-skinned Maquas had filed out of the house to watch. Young Bear joined them.

"Dirck!" He heard someone calling to him. "Dirck de Webber!"

He turned to see Hans riding toward him on a horse. Behind Hans cantered the sergeant Dirck had seen at the village landing place.

Hans slid down from his horse and rushed over. He clutched Dirck's shoulder and peered anxiously into his face. "Are you all right?" When Dirck nodded Hans scolded, "What folly! You might have drowned in the river."

Dirck set his jaw. "I was angry. I wasn't going

131

to be put into jail." Suddenly he felt a little sheepish. "I know I couldn't have gone anywhere, but I had to get away from the skipper." He rolled a stone around with the toe of his shoe.

A small frown creased Hans's high forehead. "Dirck!" he said. "You can't keep on running away from things. You have to stand on your own two feet and face up."

"Ho!" Dirck shouted. "And what have you been doing but running away?"

Hans's slender face turned white. "Well . . . well, uh," he said. "That's different. I . . . I mean I have good reason . . . to draw the Maquas and their ways."

"Boys, boys!" Jan Baptiste interrupted good-naturedly. "No quarrels right now." He turned to the sergeant who still sat his horse. "I think you are here to take Dirck back to the skipper?"

"Wooden Leg's dog!" Young Bear muttered suddenly, using the Maquas' name for General Stuyvesant's hated soldiers.

The sergeant paid no heed. He looked down at Jan Baptiste and said, "*Ja*, mynheer Director. Now Hans Kregier, bring your friend along before these smelly Wilden scalp you." He gave a wave of his dirty hand.

Jan Baptiste cleared his throat. "Ahem! Hans, I

132

see that you are too busy to greet me or your friend Young Bear. For your father's sake I'm willing to keep you boys with me a night or two. Will you agree, sergeant? I promise to deliver Dirck here for the return trip to New Amsterdam." He smiled at the boys.

The boys exchanged a quick look of hope.

"Agreed," the sergeant said at once. "I take your word as an honest man that you'll look after these two young rascals. Let the skipper bellow! Never liked him!"

With another wave of his hand, the soldier led away Hans's borrowed horse, and disappeared into the forest.

Soon Dirck was sitting in a high-backed chair close to the Van Rensselaer kitchen fire. Next to the kitchen was the large chamber with many windows overlooking the river. There Jan Baptiste carried on the business of running his vast lands.

Dirck had stopped shivering after Andries, the black servant, wrapped him in a warm blanket. It was a thicker blanket, he noticed, than the kind they traded to the Indians.

His clothes were drying fast before the warm blaze. A wild turkey browned on a spit over the coals. He sniffed hungrily.

Hans sat on a stool beside him. He was eagerly telling Dirck the plan he and Young Bear had made for the next day.

"We're going fishing, Dirck. At night!" Hans declared.

"Yes?" Dirck said. He was busy thinking about what would happen to him when he got back to New Amsterdam. How lucky he was to have run into Young Bear and Jan Baptiste at a desperate moment! But would his luck hold? He feared not.

Then he looked at Hans, whose gray eyes were shining with excitement. "How can we at night?" he wondered.

"Wait and see. Another thing . . ." Hans looked over his shoulder and lowered his voice. "Young Bear and his uncle, Great Arrow, will take me back to their town of Kaugh-na-wa-ga for a short visit. They call it a castle, and it's by the Maquas' river which flows into Hudson's River a few miles north of here. Now I can draw their camp life!"

Dirck was speechless. At last he got out, "You're going through with your plan! Mynheer Jan Baptiste expects you to return to New Amsterdam with me!"

"I started out to do this thing, and I'm going to do it," Hans said stubbornly.

Dirck nodded, suddenly understanding. "You mean you are going to stand on your own two feet. Good for you! I just hope the Maquas will let you go when you're ready."

Hans clasped his shoulder. "They will," he said with all the confidence in the world. "As soon as I have something good to show my father I'll come home. Wait for me, Dirck. Ask my father and Anneke's mother to help you."

Dirck shrugged. "I'm not sure anyone down there will help. If only I had my silver half-moon to prove who I was! But old Thomas Baxter no doubt found it at the taphouse and has it with him in Connecticut. That's where he holes in, you said?"

Hans nodded. "The rumor is that it's Fairfield, Connecticut, or New Haven."

"If only I were there!" Dirck said fiercely. "But there isn't a chance."

Just then Andries took the juicy turkey from its spit, placed it on a large pewter platter, and began to carve it. Dirck and Hans stood up, ready and waiting for their supper.

The next night Young Bear was as good as his word. Dirck and Hans joined four other visiting Maquas for a fishing trip on the river. Worried as he was, Dirck couldn't help but feel a shiver of excitement as their three elm bark canoes slipped through the smooth black water.

The Maquas, Hans told Dirck, used red elm bark for their small canoes, because they had no canoe-birch trees in their country. The elm canoes were wide and clumsy, poorly made but larger than the birch canoes the Maquas bought from other tribes.

There was plenty of room for the three boys and Lion in the canoe Young Bear used. The Maquas boy had not wished to take Lion along at first. He had never seen a dog as large as Lion.

"Be good tonight, old boy," Dirck whispered in his dog's soft ear.

The prow of their canoe, like the others, carried a flaming torch of fat pine knots. The bright fire attracted the fish and brought them close to the surface, Young Bear said in his sign language. Then they could be caught on the pronged spears each Maquas carried.

Young Bear paddled in the stern while Hans and Dirck sat in the middle of the canoe. Dirck held tightly to Lion, who wanted to jump overboard for a swim.

"Young Bear says to look sharp for the Bear-Walkers, the Night-Spirits," Hans solemnly advised Dirck.

136

Dirck laughed, almost too loudly, at this super-stition.

Shafts of light from the torches split the darkness ahead of them. The moon had not yet risen. Dirck caught glimpses of the other Wilden and heard their guttural calls. He saw them stop above an island in the center of the river and drift down with the current.

But Young Bear kept on paddling, farther and farther south. At last he reached a small island near the eastern shore. Dirck could barely see the other torches. Then they faded out.

"Aren't we rather far away?" he asked.

Hans turned and motioned to Young Bear. The boy stopped paddling. In the torchlight he made some hand signs along with a spoken Dutch word or two. He picked up his fishing spear and moved care-fully forward past the two boys. Then, using the spear shaft, he poled the canoe slowly ahead.

"He says the best fishing is by this island's shore," Hans reported. "He wants us to watch him."

Young Bear now stood there, a still figure shining with bear grease in the red torchlight. With his long spear ready, his keen eyes searched the water for a telltale gleam of a fish.

Suddenly his arm moved, the spear tip darted

137

below the surface. It broke water a second later with
a wriggling large fish on its horn points.

"*Hemel!*" Dirck breathed. "You didn't miss!"

"Perfect," Hans agreed.

Young Bear gave a pleased grunt. He pointed to
Dirck. "Dirck!" he said and handed him the spear.
Meanwhile, Lion gave a whimper of excitement and
held the flopping fish down in the bottom of the
canoe with both paws.

Dirck braced his feet as best he could in the wobbly
craft. Would he be able to pierce a fish under water
without upsetting the canoe?

He was surprised to see so many fish shadows
gathered about the light. They seemed to glow under
water. He aimed at one close to the canoe, thrust
down at it . . . and missed!

Twice more he tried, rocking the canoe until the
boys laughed. "Just once more, Hans, and then it's
your turn to try," he begged.

He waited until he saw the dim form of a big fish
near enough to reach. Drawing back the slender
fishing spear, he then plunged the points swiftly into
the fish.

The big fish struggled, while Dirck held on with
all his might. He tried to pull the spear with its
heavy burden toward him. He dropped to his knees,

138

and the rolling canoe bumped against a large rock extending from the island's shore.

The next instant the frail canoe turned over and the torch hissed out. With startled yells, Dirck and the others plunged into the river.

Dirck's head bobbed up and his feet struck bottom. The swirling water was only shoulder deep. It was not hard to wade onto the island's sandy bank.

Where were the others? "Hans . . . Young Bear, Lion," he called out through the darkness, while wiping the water from his face. He could not see the canoe. He sat on the shore and waited. Then he heard Lion's whimper and felt his nose nuzzling his wet arm.

"Good boy," Dirck said happily and hugged him close.

A sharp cry rang out, and the sounds of a scuffle came to Dirck from a short distance away. What was happening?

He stumbled forward in the direction of the noise. But now all was quiet except for . . . yes, he heard a man's breathing and Lion's warning growl.

He almost fell over someone's foot, and instantly arms of steel crushed his ribs. He struggled to free himself, kicking and biting like a savage.

At the same time he heard Lion's snarls and then

a loud howl. The man's arms slipped away from his ribs.

The man and Lion rolled in the sand. Dirck could hear them. He felt vainly for a stick or stone he could use. His fingers closed over a round stone and . . . there was a stick bound to it! An Indian war club!

He whirled and groped his way toward Lion's snarls. He found a bare shoulder with his left hand. Then he raised his right arm and brought the club down hard on the shoulder as the man started to rise to his feet.

The man gave a wild cry and fell back away from Dirck.

Answering howls came from the river. The other canoes with their torches were coming at last.

"Dirck!" Hans came toward him through the darkness. "Saint Nicholas, what's going on? I was carried down to the end of the island by the current. Where's Young Bear?"

"Here!" Dirck said tensely. He had crawled on his hands and knees until he had found Young Bear lying on the sand under a bush. "That man must have hurt him. Guard the man, Lion," he called over his shoulder. "You, too, Hans."

Lion gave a yelp in answer.

140

The moon rose above the top of the forest. Its light tinted the island beach palely, showing Dirck the oncoming canoes. It shone on Young Bear as Dirck lifted his shoulders and patted his face. Slowly the Maquas boy opened his eyes.

"Where are you hurt?" Dirck asked.

Young Bear put his hand to his head. A large lump was swelling up on the side. Dirck felt it. "No cut there," he said. "He didn't hit you squarely. You're lucky!"

Hans was hailing the other two canoes, while the strange Wild who attacked the boys sat up and groaned. Then everything seemed to be happening at once. The Maquas landed, seized and bound the prisoner, and gently lifted Young Bear into the largest canoe.

"Two of the men will stay and guard the prisoner until we can send over another canoe," Hans told Dirck excitedly. "And what do you think—he's a Mohikan, the Maquas' enemy! Must have come here to spy on Fort Orange or on the Maquas for the English."

"And we fell right into his lap!" Dirck exclaimed. "How lucky for us Lion came along tonight! You helped us catch a big fish, old boy." He patted the dog and Hans, too, came over to stroke Lion's back

141

and praise him. In a second Lion had his paws on Hans's chest and was licking his chin.

"Stop it, you big bear!" Hans, laughing, pushed him down. "I'm wet enough. Come, Dirck, they're waiting for us. Maybe by this time you're used to wet clothes, but I'm not."

Back in Van Rensselaer's house Dirck changed into dry clothes of Jan Baptiste's. Hans changed to the extra clothes he carried in his pack. Then they and Jan Baptiste went to the little guest cabin outside the stockade where the Maquas were sleeping.

They waited at the door until Cayenquirago, or Great Arrow, came out to talk. Young Bear was all right, only stunned from the Mohikan's blow, the sachem told them in broken Dutch. Tomorrow he would be well.

Then in the Maquas language Great Arrow politely thanked Dirck for coming to the aid of Young Bear.

The sachem stood proudly, his face painted in red and blue, and with a length of plaid duffel cloth draped about him. Something shone from the folds of the cloth. Dirck's eyes widened with amazement as he saw it in the dim light from the open cabin door.

Was it possible, he thought, as he sucked in his breath?

142

He stood rooted to the spot while the sachem raised his clasped hands in salute, then went inside and closed the door.

Dirck clutched Hans's arm. "Did you see it?" he asked hoarsely.

"See what?" Hans sounded puzzled.

"The chief's ornament around his neck. It couldn't be so, yet I'm sure . . . sure that he was wearing my silver half-moon!"

Suddenly Dirck's whole world seemed to turn over. He cried out in despair, "How did he get it? How will I ever get it back from a Maquas chief?"

CHAPTER ELEVEN

Gifts of the Maquas

IT WAS A BEAUTIFUL warm morning when Dirck
stepped outside Van Rensselaer's house the next day.
The tiny waves on the river sparkled in the sun. Behind the house and stable stretched a green pasture
over which horses and colts galloped. Somewhere
back in the woods a sawmill was buzzing.

Dirck, his worn jacket and breeches dried and
brushed, waited for Jan Baptiste to go with him down
to the *Sea Mew*. He looked sadly at Hans.

Hans stood tall in deerskin leggings and coat which
were decorated with seewan beads and porcupine
quills. They were a gift from Young Bear. Hans
smiled quietly at Dirck, although his eyes looked sad
at the thought of parting with his friend.

Dirck sighed and asked for the third time, "What
shall I tell your father?"

144

"Just what I've already told you. Say that I'll be home when my work is done," Hans replied.

"Don't stay long, Hans, and watch out for yourself," Dirck said in a low voice.

"I can take care of myself. Don't worry about it." Hans laughed and slapped Dirck's shoulder. "Wait for me."

Dirck didn't smile back. "Who knows what is going to happen to me when I get back to New Amsterdam? Maybe I'll never see you again." He felt in a low mood. He hated to leave with the silver half-moon so close to him.

But he knew he had to go back. Skipper Van Voort would see to that. Jan Baptiste had done all he could for Dirck, even to paying his return passage.

At that moment the Director of Rensselaerswyck rounded a corner of his house. Behind him came Young Bear and Great Arrow. Another Maquas with them carried a bundle of fur pelts.

Dirck stared at the red and blue stripes painted over the Wildens' faces and bodies. The head of an eagle stared back at him from the sachem's circle headdress of feathers. A short skirt of soft white deerskin swung over Great Arrow's high leggings, and he wore a fine blanket over all.

Dirck's eyes went back to the sachem's neck. Yes,

there shone the silver half-moon, hanging from a string of deerskin. No mistake, it was exactly like his own. It *was* his own!

Jan Baptiste looked at Dirck with a broad smile on his round face. "Dirck, the sachem wishes to thank you for saving his nephew and for helping to catch the Mohikan spy."

He nodded to Great Arrow, who stepped forward with the bearer of the fur skins. This Maquas spread them out on the ground.

"Six of the best beaver pelts I've ever seen," Jan Baptiste declared. He picked one up and handed it to Dirck.

Dirck's fingers sank into the deep fur of the pelt. He noticed that many shining rough hairs lay over the dark liver color of the outer coat. A sign, he'd heard, that the beavers were prime winter ones and not trapped "green," in the summer.

"They are all for you," the Director said, still smiling.

"For . . . for m-me?" Dirck stuttered in his astonishment. "All?" He smoothed the soft fur, while looking first at the sachem's painted face, and then over to Jan Baptiste.

"Tell the sachem thanks, mynheer, but I didn't expect this," he said. "He need not do it. Young

146

Bear pulled me out of the river and brought me to you. I helped him, too, when he was in trouble. That is all that matters."

Great Arrow spoke, while Dirck looked again at the half-moon. Then Jan Baptiste's voice was saying, "The chief insists. He will not take them back. They are yours, he says. He's very grateful. Young Bear is his sister's child and his heir, because the chieftains are chosen from the woman's side of the family."

Almost as in a dream, Dirck replied, "Tell him I'll trade all the beavers back to him for the silver medal he's wearing. It once belonged to me and my family. It means a great deal to me. I do not know how he got it way up here. I lost it in New Amsterdam many days ago."

"Eh? You did? *Hemel!*" Jan Baptiste looked startled. He talked again to Great Arrow.

Dirck held his breath. How had he ever had the courage to ask for it? "Nothing tried, nothing gained." He could almost hear Long Mary saying that. Maybe it would work.

Great Arrow stared for a time at Dirck. He raised his long fingers to the cord around his neck. He hesitated, then slowly untied it and held the medal in his palm.

148

"Do you have proof that the silver medal belongs to you?" Jan Baptiste asked.

"Yes, mynheer," Dirck stepped forward eagerly. "The year 1609 and my name, de Webber, are cut into the back of it. Also, Hendrik Hudson's name. My great-uncle was a mate on the ship *The Half-Moon*. Hendrik Hudson gave him the medal as a keepsake of their discovery of New Netherlands."

Hesitantly, Dirck turned over the half-moon lying on the chief's yellow palm. "See there." He pointed to the carved letters with shaking fingers.

"*Hemel*, yes!" The Director leaned over and read the letters. He nodded to Great Arrow and said, "It is so. The writing says it." He repeated his words in the Maquas tongue.

Great Arrow gravely spoke to them at some length. Then he placed the silver medal in Dirck's hand. He said a few more words to the delighted boy. He swept his arm toward the beavers and strode away with his tribesman at his heels.

"Dirck!" Hans cried. "He's giving you the beavers, too. What luck! He's most generous for a Maquas."

Dirck was so happy he could hardly stand it. He brushed the smooth silver with his fingertips and read again the writing on the back. He looked at

Jan Baptiste with dazed eyes. "Both for me? And how did he get the half-moon from so far away? I don't understand."

Jan Baptiste smiled. "He doesn't want to keep what belongs to the brave lad, he says. It seems he sent two runners through the enemy Mohikan lands to the English settlements at the sea. They carried parcels of furs to trade.

"But their real purpose was to seek out a tribesman who had been captured by the Mohikans and sold in Connecticut as a slave. The runners, of course, were to avoid being seen by the Mohikans.

"They quietly searched in the villages near the sea, but found no trace of their tribesman. Several days ago a ship captain's silver pin caught the eye of one of the runners, and he offered two beavers for it. The trade was made, and the Maquas ran back through the forests with it. They brought the half-moon pin to their chief yesterday in place of their lost tribesman."

Dirck shook his head. "Who ever would believe I'd find my half-moon way up here in this wilderness? Those Wilden must have run more than fifty miles in a day! It surely is the hand of God, mynheer."

Hans interrupted, "Maybe a Mohikan stumbled

over the Maquas runners' trail and so was spying on us at the island. Here, let me see the medal, Dirck. Just think, the great Hudson once held it in his hand!"

Dirck gave it to the eager Hans. He walked over with a smile to Young Bear who had been sharing the excitement. He held out his hand. "You'll never know how glad I am that I met you, Young Bear. You are a good friend, and I thank you and your uncle for these gifts."

Young Bear's dark eyes brightened and a rare smile lighted his handsome face. He gripped Dirck's hand and managed a "*Ja*, *ja*, Dirck. Friend."

Dirck wished he had something to give Young Bear.

He stepped over to the pile of large beaverskins and took one. He gave it to Young Bear. "To repay you for the beavers given for the silver half-moon," he said, and Jan Baptiste repeated the words.

Young Bear nodded and said he would keep the beaver.

"We must hurry, Dirck," the Director said quickly. "Skipper Van Voort is waiting for us and the tide will soon turn. He'll be sending after you in a minute."

"Yes, mynheer, and I'll remember you always for

all you've done for me," Dirck replied, clasping Jan Baptiste's hand.

It was time to go, and Dirck hated to leave Hans. He was almost afraid to face the unknown in New Amsterdam. Would they accept his proof as to who he was? Would he soon find a way to go home to Rotterdam?

He would know the answer in a few days.

Thoughts of home filled Dirck's mind all the way south on the river. He was glad it was a fast trip. They stayed in the center of the river where the current was strongest. Both wind and tide favored them as they swept downstream toward the bay and ocean.

Dirck was careful to keep himself and Lion out of the skipper's way as much as possible. While Claes and Van Voort knew about the beaverskins, Dirck did not tell them about his silver crescent.

The skipper had little to say, but he often cast dark looks at Dirck. Remembering what had happened at Fort Orange, Dirck made a plan of action. As soon as the *Sea Mew's* rowboat neared the dock, he planned to jump over to it before the skipper could stop him.

Then, his pack of furs under his arm, he would run to the house of Hans's father. He would explain everything to Captain Kregier and have his help when he went before the Town Council for a permit to sail. He would offer his beavers as payment for a passage to the Netherlands.

He laughed out loud at the thought. Then he stopped and brushed back the hair from his face. The wind and sun were strong on the river.

It must be past May Day, he thought. I've been gone from home such a long time. Dear Mother and Father and Marie and little Piet, I miss you! I'll be a better brother when I get back.

The afternoon of the third day they passed the Spuyten Duyvil Creek, on the northern tip of Man-hattes Island. Dirck knew they would soon be in port.

Boats were crossing the wide bay and river. He passed Anneke's fine house where the green grass sloped to the high river bluff from the blossoming orchard. Then he saw the belfry and twin gables of Saint Nicholas church above the trees.

The *Sea Mew* rounded the end of the island where the fort stood guard, and at last anchored in the East River at the landing place. Overhead Dirck saw a black thunderhead which threatened an early rain.

He and Lion sat in the bow of the rowboat while the skipper rowed to shore. His bundle of furs lay at his feet. On a sudden impulse he took his silver half-moon from his breeches pocket and hung it about his neck. He would wear it proudly when he faced New Amsterdam.

"Make fast the line," the skipper ordered as they neared the little dock. Dirck picked up the line and his bundle at the same time. He stood up, his leg muscles tense. Suddenly he dropped the line and jumped over the narrow space of water. He landed safely on the dock. Lion jumped after him, a second later.

"Stop!" roared Skipper Van Voort, as he chopped at the water with his oars.

Dirck took to his heels. He threaded through the sailors, porters and fisherfolk who stood on shore. A glance over his shoulder told him that the skipper was climbing out of the boat now, bent on following him.

He ran swiftly past the brick business houses on the waterfront. He knew where there was a tiny lane going through to the next road inland. Just a few more steps, and he darted into it, brushing past a man in sailor's clothes. Dirck hoped that passersby did not take notice of him.

154

The ground in this narrow way was damp and slippery. A mist began to rise through the fading light. Soon he came out into Brugh Street, the street of the canal bridge. Lion, who had run ahead, stopped and waited.

A quick turn to his left and there was Winkel Lane, only twelve feet wide. Along its left side were several houses facing the fort with their backs to the lane. On the right were five old warehouses built together, and now mostly empty.

"In here, Lion," Dirck ordered and he let the dog run on ahead.

He had taken only a few steps into Winkel Lane when he felt a hand grip his shoulder. It jerked him back into the doorway of an empty warehouse.

"Ach! what . . ." he started to say. Before he could get the words out he was pulled through a door into the dark inside. It took only an instant.

The door slammed shut as he struggled to loosen the grip around his neck. He heard Lion yelp and throw himself against the door.

The strong hand loosened its grip and Dirck gasped for breath. "That'll fix you," a coarse voice said in his ear.

"Who . . . who are you?" Dirck said. Who was this man? He kept his face in the shadows.

155

The man's hand tore the silver half-moon from Dirck's neck. "The duyvil only knows how you found this silver piece! Blast my scuppers, but Captain Baxter will be pleased to see it again!"

The man moved into the pale beam of light from a dusty window. Dirck made out a cruel face with a flat nose and a gold earring.

"You are . . . you are the one called Flips," he blurted out.

"Right you are! Sorry I can't take you with me, swabber, so you won't bleat that I was here," Flips snarled. "Now cut your cables! I'll take course to another harbor."

Outside Lion was barking mightily, and Dirck heard voices at the door.

Suddenly Flips seemed to melt back into the dark shadows. Dirck ran to the door and unlatched it. Two men stood outside with Lion, who leaped upon Dirck with whimpers of joy.

"What's coming about in there?" one of the burghers demanded. "This dog was making a great noise."

"A sailor dragged me into this building and stole the silver medal I was wearing!" Dirck shook the man's arm excitedly. "Quick! Can't someone go after him?"

"Are you all right? And do you know who he was?" the other man asked.

"Oh, I'm all right now. Yes, he's Flips, one of the pirate Baxter's men." Dirck said hurriedly. "Maybe he's still inside somewhere . . ."

"Ach! Thomas Baxter's in Connecticut, our sea patrol reports. He couldn't be here. It must have been another," the first man said. He peered into the dark building, but made no move to enter. He seemed anxious to go since Dirck appeared unhurt.

Dirck didn't feel like arguing. Flips was gone by now.

Just then large drops of rain began to spatter their faces. "Report it to the burgherguard," one of the men said over his shoulder, as they rushed back to their houses across the lane.

Dirck found his fur bundle lying by the warehouse door. A lump came to his throat as he picked it up. His precious silver half-moon gone again!

He gritted his teeth angrily. I'll get it back, he vowed. I won't leave the New World without my silver half-moon.

The rain poured down while he ran through puddles and mud to the end of Winkel Lane. He turned past Jansen the baker's, and came to the Marckveldt Road and the north wall of the fort.

157

Both streets seemed empty, with no sign of Flips or of Skipper Van Voort.

He ran up the Marckveldt to the open green before the fort. Across it he could see the lights in the windows of the Kregier Inn and the houses on each side of it. He hoped Captain Kregier would take him in.

He lifted the inn's brass knocker and dropped it back against the divided door. Soon the top part of it was unlatched and a red-cheeked woman looked out.

"Please may I see Captain Kregier?" Dirck said.

"You want lodging?" the housekeeper demanded, peering at him from under a large white cap. "If so, go 'round to the back door. I can't have you muddying my clean floors."

"No, I'm not a guest. But I *have* to see the Captain. It's very important," Dirck said desperately.

The woman frowned at him. "Captain Kregier is out of town. Come back in a few days."

A few days! Dirck's heart sank. While he stood there, tonguetied and wet, the housekeeper closed the top of the Dutch door firmly. It was plain to see she wanted no muddy waif in her kitchen.

Why had he said nothing of Hans? What a dunce he was!

He knocked again, but the woman wouldn't answer.

Dirck placed his hand on Lion, who stood patiently beside him. He looked from the closed door up the hill to his right. Up there was the cemetery and past it was Anneke's house. Would he find a warmer welcome there?

He squared his shoulders and started forward. "Never mind, old boy," he said to Lion. "We have another place to try . . . before jail."

But he gathered strength and forced his tired legs to trot up Heere Street, past the workers' small houses on his right and the empty lots on his left. He went on past the gate of the old cemetery and followed a white fence to Anneke's fine stone-faced house with its high gabled roof.

This time he didn't go to the front door. He stumbled through a gate in the dusk and around to the back of the house. He found a doorknocker and dropped it loudly.

The rain stopped just then, and in the sudden quiet he heard a gay voice. "Maybe it's Father!" The door was flung open.

Anneke, her face alight, stood before him. Her gaze met his in surprise, and the light faded from her face.

159

"It's not he, Mother," she said slowly. Then she smiled and cried out, "*Ach*, I know who you are now! You're so wet you look like a drowned chicken, Dirck NoName. Come in! We thought you had run away." She opened the door wide.

"Wait in the stable, Lion," Dirck ordered over his shoulder. He slipped off his muddy, broken shoes by the door.

"Anneke, I've been to Fort Orange with Hans. He's still there and I have no place to go," he said as he stepped inside.

This large comfortable kitchen with its brick floor looked like heaven. Its scrubbed-white ceiling beams and big fireplace with blue tiled borders was much like his own back in Rotterdam.

His quick glance took in a Holland cupboard of nutwood which held pewter plates, silver pieces and earthenware. On the wall, wood racks held silver spoons, pewter mugs, and knives. Besides the square table and its benches, there were several rush-seated chairs.

He suddenly noticed that Vrouw Van der Grift, plump and smiling, stood before him.

"Mother," Anneke was saying, "this is the poor shipwrecked boy I told you about. I'm sure he is a lost prince, maybe. We must help him, please?"

160

"Prince, eh?" Her mother laughed and shook her head at Anneke. "Such a girl!" But Dirck saw that her eyes were kind as she looked at him. She wore a fine brown linen dress with a long pointed bodice, and slashed and puffed sleeves. From a silver chain around her waist hung scissors, thimble, keys, and a pincushion.

Suddenly the room began to spin around. Dirck's legs felt rubbery and his head ached. He dropped his bundle of furs and felt a chair being pushed under him. Motherly hands took off his wet jacket, and the bundle was placed in a corner.

Anneke brought dry clothes from a large chest. She said they belonged to her older brother, Gerrit, who was a student at the college in Leyden, Holland.

As Dirck tried to swallow a little bread and milk, he told them about his trip to Fort Orange with Hans and about the silver half-moon and how he had recovered his memory.

Vrow Van der Grift clucked over Dirck's mishaps, while Anneke exclaimed excitedly as she listened.

"I'm very glad your memory has come back," she said, smiling at him. "You'll get home again, never fear." She said this with more faith than Dirck had.

"We were worried over Hans's leaving while his

father was away," she declared. "Their horrid housekeeper wouldn't tell us he left a letter."

"*Ja,*" said her mother. "Now when Mynheer Kregier comes back we will have news of Hans for him. But to live with the fierce Maquas! Hans is a wooden-head. *Ach*, here we sit talking when the poor lad can't keep his eyes open."

She called upstairs for their servant Lintie to come down and ready the kitchen betse, the cupboard bed, for Dirck. Meanwhile Anneke ran out to the stable with food for the patient Lion.

Dirck rolled into the soft featherbed, and was asleep as soon as his aching head touched the big square pillow.

CHAPTER TWELVE

The Bouwerie

A ROOSTER CROWED to the dawn, and a cow lowed out in the Van der Grift stable. Light streamed through the two small glass panes in the kitchen windows and touched Dirck's eyes.

He opened them slowly. For a moment things blurred, and his head ached. He thrust his fingers into his thick yellow hair and touched the newly healed scar there.

"Where am I?" he muttered, looking around the large room. Then he remembered last night. "It must be that I'm really safe in Anneke's house."

He lay still and stared at the wide fireplace with its hourglass and silver candlesticks. There was a ruffle of wavy striped cloth, called tabby cloth, hanging along the mantle edge above the ash-covered fire. In Rotterdam, his mother always hung a fresh tabby

163

cloth ruffle along their kitchen mantle every Saturday. On the hearth lay the tin box of flints, scorched linen and pine splinters ready to start a fire.

Dirck grinned suddenly when he saw the four posts and cross beams of a small hand loom filling one corner, for it had an unfinished piece of weaving on it. How many times he had slipped away from an unfinished piece in his father's shop . . . slipped away to go boating on the canals, pretending he was an explorer in search of new lands!

Then his smile faded when he remembered one of the times last winter Father had been disappointed in him. That was when Father had sent him on an errand to the Groote Markt, the big market, to pick up an engraving done by the local artist Rembrandt.

Instead, Dirck had gone off gaily skating on the frozen canal, and by the time he reached the market, the engraving was sold.

"Dirck'll never make a dependable master weaver," he had overheard one of his Father's weavers say with a shake of the head.

Then Dirck had laughed, but this morning he felt an uneasy wish he could have changed all that.

The morning church bells began to ring, and he sat up on the edge of the betse. The room swam before him. He fell back on the checked linen pillow for a

164

moment. What was wrong with him? His head felt so queer and his throat was sore.

He heard sounds upstairs and forced himself to dress quickly. Now footsteps tapped down the stairs. He heard a cheery "Good morrow."

Anneke's mother and her fat servant Lintie bustled into the room, smiling their good mornings at him. They carried bundles and boxes which they carefully set down at the back door. For the first time Dirck noticed hampers of food near the kettles at the hearth.

"And how are you today?" Anneke's mother asked briskly.

"Well enough . . . I think," Dirck muttered. But he thought the room was very hot. He sat on the edge of his bed. "Are you going away, Mevrouw Van der Grift?"

"We're going to our farm at Sapokanican," Anneke sang out. She ran into the kitchen with her little quilted cap slipping over one ear. "For two whole weeks! We didn't tell you last night . . ." She stopped still and stared at Dirck, who was resting his head in his hands.

"What's wrong?" she and her mother asked at the same time.

"He looks ill." Her mother frowned. She went over and placed a plump hand on Dirck's forehead.

"He's burning with fever. Perhaps we should call Surgeon Kierstede. Anneke, go over to his house and bring him back."

"Yes, Mother," Anneke replied and sped away, not listening to Dirck's reply that it was nothing.

Soon she returned with the news that the surgeon had gone out to see a sick person. He might come in the afternoon.

"We'll be gone this afternoon," her mother said. "Yet we can't leave him here, sick and alone. Even though Lintie is returning with Simon Congo tonight."

"I'll be all right soon," Dirck promised them. "I can find a place to stay. I'll trade a beaver for bed and board until I can get passage on a ship for home."

Anneke tossed her head, and her cap slipped farther over her ear. "*Ach*, yes! If Skipper Van Voort doesn't make more trouble for you. Or some of the townspeople, who say you helped Sam Low trade with the pirates and steal beavers from the Wilden. And they say that your big black pirate dog killed and ate sheep in the commons outside the wall."

"Lion?" gasped Dirck. He shook his head to clear it. "Lion wouldn't do that. It must have been wolves. None of that is true, I swear."

"Just the same, Schout Van Ten's been looking for you since you went away. It seems a man gave him a note that you had carried to Captain Baxter from Sam Low. Then Sam disappeared before he could be banished as a traitor. So Schout Van Ten's angry about that. If he sees you and you don't have the silver half-moon to show who you are . . ." she spread out her hands with a shrug of her shoulders.

Dirck groaned in despair. His silver crescent! He couldn't go away without it, even if he escaped the anger of the townsfolk. "What can I do? If only Uncle Nick were alive!" He rubbed his forehead as he felt a wave of heat beat against his brain.

Anneke ran over to her mother who had just come back into the kitchen.

"Mother," he heard her whisper. "Don't you see? We must take Dirck to the farm with us. If he has a slight chill, it will go away soon. He will feel better after a rest there, and he'll be safe from that hateful sheriff. Then we can plan a way to help him see General Stuyvesant. Please? He can help at the farm, too."

The good-hearted Vrouw looked thoughtfully at Dirck.

He felt uncomfortable under her gaze and made a great effort to stand up. "I must look after Lion,"

167

he told them. He tottered toward the door. Lion was still tied in the stable and he could hear him barking.

"Mother!" Anneke softly begged and clung to her arm.

Suddenly her mother nodded, and the little pearls in her ears bobbed. "Yes, there's no other way. What must be, must be! Dirck, you are to go with us. It is settled. Lintie, tell Simon Congo to start loading the farm wagon."

Dirck was whisked out to the farm wagon. There he sat on a feather mattress while Simon Congo piled boxes and baskets around him. Just enough room was left for Anneke and her mother to ride in back with him.

Simon would drive the two horses. Lintie, looking like a pumpkin in her green bodice and orange petticoats, sat in front beside him. Lion could follow behind the wagon.

The wagon crept through marshes and over sand hills. It bounced over the old Wilden trail higher into dense woods of hickory. Even the mattress couldn't soften the jolts for Dirck's aching head.

He hardly knew when they turned off the main trail about a half-hour later. They rode on through partly cleared woods.

168

"There's our spring where we get water," he heard Anneke sing out. And soon, "There's our farm in the woods, our Bossen Bouwerie. It looks just the same, Mother."

The wagon jolted to a stop in a wide grassy glen. Dirck caught a glimpse of a stone farmhouse with a deep sloping roof of shingles. The woods almost touched it on one side, while on the other side was a large barn for the Holstein cattle.

Three thatched cottages of the tenant farmers faced the house across the open space. Cattle sheds were built onto the backs of the cottages. Dirck was hardly aware of all this now.

He felt Simon Congo's strong arms carrying him into the house. He was put down and covered up.

Much, much later he heard Anneke's mother speak in a low tone. "His face is breaking out in a rash. Let us hope it is not the pox!"

"Don't fear, mistress," another woman answered in a voice he knew. "I say, a sad welcome is better than a sad farewell." A cold wet cloth was slapped on his forehead.

Who could mistake that cracked voice? It must be, it could be none other than Long Mary!

"How'd you come here? Why?" he mumbled and tried to see her with his bleary eyes. Long Mary's face swam before him. Her stringy gray hair was caught back under a clean white cap.

"Heh, heh!" she cackled. "Your kind friends helped an old lady. When Sam Low disappeared and General Stuyvesant took over his house, I had no place to go. I live here and take care of the farmhouse. But that can wait. Hold your tongue, boy, and save your breath."

Dirck remembered the *Sea Mew's* mate, Claes. "I caught this fever from the sick mate on the *Sea Mew*, I think. It's not the pox." Now they need not be afraid of him.

The next two days Dirck's body burned with a high fever. By this time he was entirely covered with a red rash. When his fever broke, it left him weak and white. All the while he had been watched over by Long Mary.

Weak as he was, Dirck could still marvel at the change in Long Mary's appearance. A neat white kerchief was folded about her thin neck. Her full gray skirts were pinned back over a new blue petticoat. Even her thin face and hooked nose looked less "witchy" under her clean Dutch cap. How wonderful the Van der Grift's have been to two strays, he thought!

Anneke stole into his little room the first day he

sat up in bed. He was watching the forest birds in a green tree outside his tiny window, his hand on Lion's black head.

"Hurry up and get well, Dirck," she urged. "The May flowers are blooming. The farmers are planting." She dropped down onto a little stool and straightened her thin linen cap. Today she wore her pale gold hair loose down her back.

"I'm glad you have helped Long Mary," he answered.

"We didn't tell you . . . I wanted it to be a surprise." She smiled at him. "Wasn't it?" she giggled.

"It was that." He smiled back at her.

Then she eagerly told him about the new young lambs and the tenant farmers' roly-poly babies . . . and that a small tribe of the Wappinger Indians was back in summer camp from north of the Spuyten Duyvil creek. They raised corn in a fertile meadow beside Hudson's river, and also dried fish for their winter's needs.

Dirck listened to her and nodded. "I would like to see their camp." Then he said softly. "It's so different from Holland. There are a few kind people in the New Netherlands, after all. I thank you and your mother for being good to me, a stranger. And to Lion, too."

Anneke smiled happily. "Mother says we must help others in need. Besides, I wanted to do it. I love Lion." She threw her arms about the dog's neck and hugged him, knocking off her cap as she did so.

Dirck had to laugh, hearing Lion's tail thump on the floor. "He likes you, too."

Then he motioned to the window. "The birds out there make me think of Hans. Why did he have to go so far away, Anneke, when a camp of Wilden is near here? And is he safe? I wonder about him."

"He will be safe if he's Van Rensselaer's friend." She wandered over to the window. "And he did visit our meadow Wilden last summer with us. He drew a whole book of wonderful sketches. His father frowned and barely glanced at them. Hans felt bad. He wants to draw like Mynheer Rembrandt, the artist in Holland."

"Poor Hans!" Dirck sighed, remembering how patient his father, Joris, had been with his selfish whims. "When I return home, I'll go back to Latin School gladly," he declared.

"We had a Latin School for older young people last year and hope to soon again," she said. "I've been through our public school. Master Verstisius is teaching the younger children in a rented house this year. Did you know that they don't have a public school in the New England colonies?" she said proudly. Then, strangely shy, she added, "It would be pleasant to have you stay and go to Latin School here, too."

"I wish I could!" Dirck surprised himself by saying.

His strength began to come back quickly, once he went outside into the warm May sunshine.

In the days that followed, he and Anneke often wandered along the forest's ancient Wilden trails. Grapevines hung in thick festoons from the large forest trees. The vines added their fragrance to the delicate scent of strange wild flowers and white-blooming fruit trees.

Everything here smells fresh and green and wonderful, Dirck thought.

On their walks they delighted in teaching Lion commands in Dutch. After a time, Anneke exclaimed, "I think he understands every word we say!"

Once Lion went away, only to return dragging a wild turkey, proud in its purple feathers. "Who needs a gun or bow and arrow?" Dirck laughed, as he stroked Lion's glossy back.

Together they helped the farmers drive the black-and-white cows from the woods before dusk. Dirck even helped the farmers set out the young tobacco plants in a cleared field and meadow. Tobacco was the chief crop of this farm in the woods.

One of the farmer's wives gave him a blue linen shirt-coat the color of Anneke's blue apron. With red leather breeches, he wore a sleeveless brown jerkin of linsey-woolsy. The farmer's buskins suited him better than wooden shoes, he declared. The buskins had leather soles with sides of cloth which were laced up his legs to his knees.

Dirck had hoped to visit the camp of the Wappingers several miles north of them, especially since a Wild youth came with an invitation from the chief. In spite of Dirck's eager urging, Mevrouw van der Grift refused to go.

"Anneke's father would not want us to go without a grown man along," she said firmly. "Our farmers are too busy to go with us." Instead, she sent back gifts of a smoked ham and hen's eggs, foods the chief dearly loved.

Dirck was disappointed. He wanted to see the dome-shaped bark lodges these people of the Algonquin race lived in. He wanted to watch the men make a canoe by hollowing out a great log with burn-

174

ing and scraping. But Anneke's mother would not allow him to go there alone, and he didn't wish to disobey her.

Toward the end of the month he grew restless. They had extended their stay, and it was four weeks now since he had come to the Bossen Bouwerie. In the back of his mind burned the thought that he must try to find his silver half-moon again. He couldn't do that here on the farm.

He had his beavers to pay his passage home. Surely there would be a ship coming soon, one that was going back again to Holland.

Do I dare go back to town if Schout Van Ten is still looking for me, he wondered. Can Anneke's mother protect me from the angry townspeople? I'll just have to take that chance.

On the last day of May Simon Congo appeared for his weekly load of logs. No, he told Vrouw Van der Grift, there still was no word of her husband's yacht, so long overdue. But there was bad news from the New England plantations.

A fleet of English ships was in Boston, ready to attack the Dutch! The whole town was alarmed, he said.

They all stared at each other in dismay.

"We must go back to town at once," decided the

good Vrouw Van der Grift firmly. "I must guard our valuables and our house. *Ach*, New Netherlands needs my husband's cargo more than ever now. May the good Lord send him in time!"

"No, mistress," Long Mary cried out. "Please stay here. You'll be safer if the English come. Remember . . . out of sight, out of mind!"

Vrouw Van der Grift gave Long Mary a gentle smile and patted her arm. "You may stay here as long as you wish, if you think the English might still have ideas about your being a witch. You can gather and dry fresh herbs in the forest. However, I believe they won't capture Fort Amsterdam." She pressed her lips together. "We leave as soon as we're packed."

Then Dirck found himself surrounded with a mighty hustle and bustle. Everyone scurried around to collect belongings and farm products to take back.

After he had done all he could to help, he carried his own bundle out to the wagon. He felt proud of the new clothes he wore. The good Vrouw and Long Mary had made him wide breeches and shirt and a slashed-sleeved jacket with many buttons, all from the Captain's larger ones.

Just at he was trying to find room for his bundle, Lion gave a sharp bark of warning. Dirck heard a

176

horse galloping up the wagon trail through the woods. Then a soldier in a plumed helmet rode into the open flat.

"It's Hans's father," he heard Anneke squeal in excitement behind him.

She rushed over to Captain Kregier as he got off his horse. She bobbed a curtsy. "Welcome, Mynheer," she said. "Mother will be out at once."

The Captain's hard gray eyes swept over Dirck. "Simon Congo and Lintie tell me that this lad has news of Hans. I've had my skipper's report. Now I want to talk to this boy."

Anneke introduced Dirck. The Captain asked him many questions about their trip to Fort Orange and Hans's visit to the Maquas. His stern face grew sad as he said, "The Maquas are cruel to their prisoners. How could Hans risk his life?"

Dirck explained as best he could. "Hans is their guest, not a prisoner. He went as a friend of Young Bear's, who will be the next sachem of the Bear clan, as you know. He wanted to prove to you . . ."

"He chose to go off to the Wilden instead of living at home with me," Captain Kregier interrupted.

Dirck was amazed to see bright tears in the man's eyes. Suddenly he felt sorry for the Captain. He

177

understood how his own father must have felt when he ran off.

He shook his head. "No, Mynheer Kregier. Hans wanted to prove to you that he was a man, even if he didn't want to be a soldier or a trader. He wanted to draw the Maquas and their way of life. Something that may be valued years from now . . . when there are many of us and few Wilden in this country. He hopes to make you proud of him, Mynheer Captain, but in his own way."

Captain Kregier bent his head. He slapped the horse's reins into his palm thoughtfully. Finally he looked up. "*Ach*, the boy's been lonesome since his mother's gone. I must talk more to him when he comes back . . . if he comes."

Dirck grinned. "He should be back soon. He planned to spend only a few weeks with Young Bear. He promised me he would come back."

"Good, good! I'll send my sloop up to get him." The Captain chuckled in relief and scratched his dark beard. "Now tell me about yourself, Dirck."

Anneke, her mother and Long Mary all helped Dirck tell Captain Kregier about his adventures in the New World. When they finished the Captain promised his protection to Dirck.

"You've heard the bad news?" he added as he

mounted his horse. "Isaac Allerton, our Puritan merchant friend, has sent a warning to the city from Massachusetts. It seems the English colonies wrote to Oliver Cromwell, who has made himself the ruler of England. They asked Cromwell to send them ships and men to attack us."

"Simon just came to tell us. Then it's true?" Anneke's mother said anxiously.

Hans's father nodded. "Of course, we've heard rumors often, but this time it is true. A shipload of soldiers has arrived in Boston, the first of four, Mynheer Allerton writes. Connecticut and Rhode Island Plantations are raising men to fight us. Even Plymouth, which was against war, has raised fifty men under Captain Miles Standish."

"We're leaving for home at once," Vrouw Van der Grift said. "We have so few soldiers. What can we do against so many?" She looked worried in spite of herself.

"All of the townspeople have worked hard to improve our fort and wall," Captain Kregier answered grimly. "We've called up a militia of sixty men. Neither the West India Company nor the Netherlands government will help us. We will do our best to fight for our freedom. You know our need for gunpowder."

179

With that he saluted and rode off, the plume on his helmet bobbing wildly.

Yes, Dirck knew their need for powder, which was the lost Captain Van der Grift's cargo from the West Indies. He knew, too, that if the English attacked soon, there would not be enough powder to fight back!

CHAPTER THIRTEEN

Escape

ALARMING REPORTS raced about town during the month of June. One day Dirck would hear, "A thousand soldiers are on the way!" . . . the next, "No, they're waiting for three more ships from England."

Soon he heard, "There's treason! The English settlers on Long Island are helping the English privateers." All this time there was still no word of Captain Paulus Van der Grift's missing yacht with its load of gunpowder.

The people were too worried over the coming attack to take much notice of Dirck. He was careful to stay out of Sheriff Van Ten's sight, though.

Throughout the excitement he waited for a ship bound for home. He made a dozen plans to find pirate Baxter and his silver half-moon before leaving. But what chance did he really have now of going to Connecticut to look for it? Trading between the Dutch and English colonies had come to a standstill.

Hans, strong and tanned, came back safely from his Maquas visit, much to his father's relief. He brought back a stack of excellent sketches and wonderful tales. This time Captain Kregier showed he was proud of his son, and Hans seemed to Dirck more sure of himself. Now Dirck divided his time between Hans's and Anneke's homes.

He and Hans stopped at the waterside early one morning to look out at the two-masted yacht *King Solomon*. It was riding at anchor between Manhattes Island and Long Island. It had come from Brazil a few days before.

"If only General Stuyvesant *would* let her sail," Dirck mourned, eyeing the high decked stern with its fancy gilded carvings. At the top of her mainmast the red, white and blue flag of the Netherlands Republic hung limp in the sun.

He frowned. "I know my family's worried. It's been almost six months since poor Uncle Nicholas and I left home . . . and no word from us."

"Sail?" Hans gave a short laugh. "How can she? Part of her crew jumped ship in Virginia. She has no gunners and no powder. Father says what good are naval victories in Europe, if the company or the government sends us no supplies? They say that Captain Van der Grift's ship is lost."

Dirck sighed. "Anneke and her mother have not given up hope." He picked up a pebble and skipped it across the water. "Maybe something will happen to save him and save our town."

Hans shrugged his shoulder and looked gloomy. "It would be a miracle. Even Father says so. We don't have more than two hundred men to fight." Suddenly a smile lit his face. "Father talks over everything with me now," he added happily. "I'm trying harder to please him, too."

"I'm glad," Dirck said. "Tell me, Hans, how do you show someone you're sorry?"

"By saying so or something like it." Hans stared at him.

"Saying, 'sorry' isn't enough. Not when you've run away and made your family feel bad," Dirck said. "I think . . . I think it has to be more . . . like saying 'forgive me' and showing them you feel bad, too, and won't do it again. Being away off here has made me see how selfish I was, how thoughtless of everyone else. I hope I've learned to stand on my own two feet, too. I'm even going to be nicer to my little brother and sister," he added in a generous mood.

Hans laughed. "By Saint Nicholas, Dirck! You sound like our preacher, Domine Megapolensis."

Dirck flushed and laughed, too. "Oh, think no more of it!"

Just the same, he felt he had failed his family by not recovering the silver crescent.

"We'd do well to hurry." He heard Hans's warning voice. "If we don't, you'll be too late to get your permit to sail home!" Dirck wanted to get it before the Town Council held Monday law court.

It was Monday, market day. Farmers' and fishers' boats from Long Island, Staten Island, and the west Hudson shores were pulled up on the bank. "Over here for fresh fish, oysters, lobsters." "Fresh greens, wild strawberries, cheeses." They all called their wares.

Dirck looked about for old Kryn the oysterman. He was sure Kryn would like to know what had happened since the old fellow rescued him.

"Hurry! There are the drums! They're coming now," Hans cried and started to run. "We'll be too late."

The town councilmen were marching up the wide stone steps of the Town Hall. Two drummers led

184

the group. Next came the flagbearer, then the court messenger and his helpers, carrying the red cushions of state for the Council.

After them strutted Schout Cornelis Van Ten, the two burgomasters, Martin Kregier and Arent Van Hattem, and the four schepens, all in black hats with silver bands. Director-General Pieter Stuyvesant and the state officials were missing, since they usually did not attend the Town Council meetings.

Knots of passersby stood around to watch this impressive parade.

The boys followed the group inside. They went down the hall past the leather firebuckets hanging on the wall, up the curving stairs to the second floor courtroom. Across the hall at the back, Dirck got a quick look at the jailroom.

Inside the courtroom, Hans caught his father's eyes. Burgomaster Kregier motioned the boys up to the judge's bench. Dirck explained his business to the magistrates. He told them he had recovered his memory, and wished to return home on the next ship that sailed. He said he had money from the sale of his fine beavers to pay his passage.

Schout Van Ten, who sat at the head of the Council, listened while his face grew ever redder. Finally he burst out with, "*Hemel*, we have only this young ruffian's word as to who he is. How do we know if these beavers were given to him? That tapster swore that Dirck acted as go-between for Sam Low and the pirates. He should also pay for the sheep his pirate dog killed in the commons." He rattled his sword hilt with his fat fingers and blew out his lips. "There is treason here within our wall! I demand that the boy be punished!"

A chill ran down Dirck's spine. He stood frozen and speechless.

"Worshipful Lord, we have Dirck's word that he did not willingly work for the pirates. You yourself put the boy into the traitor Sam Low's hands." Burgomaster Kregier spoke icily. He continued, "Kryn, the oysterman of Oyster Bay, just now sends word to me that he's found wreckage with the English name 'Desire' painted on it. It could be the English sloop Thomas Baxter and his crew stole from the English settlement at Hempstede, and on which Dirck was wrecked. Nicholas de Webber *was* lost in the storm, as far as we can find out."

Dirck hung his head sadly, while Martin Kregier moved some papers about. "Ah, here it is! Our clerk has a list of passengers aboard the yacht *Gilded Beaver*, who are being held in Rhode Island. The governor there promises to return them soon. Un-

186

fortunately, Dirck's uncle's name, Nicholas de Webber, is not on the list."

Martin Kregier leaned forward and glared back into Schout Van Ten's scowling face. "Even this boy's fine dog has been unjustly accused," he declared. The other councilmen listened closely. They stared at Lion, who was sitting quietly at Dirck's heel. "Yesterday afternoon Gabriel the herder caught a wolf-dog eating a sheep. The dog belonged to a fat boy named Goosen. I say belonged, because the burgherwatch shot him."

"Thunder and lightning!" Dirck gulped and felt Hans squeeze his arm. He was glad they knew now it wasn't Lion, but he was sorry about Goosen's dog.

Hans's father still was not done. "As to the beavers the boy sold . . . both my skipper Van Voort and my son tell me it is true a Maquas sachem gave them to the boy. I could have Jan Baptiste Van Rensselaer send word from Fort Orange about this, but I think my two witnesses are enough. And you, Mynheer Van Ten, know the truth of all this!"

The fiery schout growled in his throat.

Burgomaster Kregier's hard eyes flashed. "You hunted out Long Mary at the Bossen Bouwerie and tried to make her say the boy had long worked for the pirate Baxter. But she refused to be a witness for you.

187

She said it was untrue, that the pirate had kidnapped Dirck when they captured the *Gilded Beaver*."

Dirck grinned suddenly and burst out with "Good old Long Mary!" He realized that without her and the council, Van Ten could do little against him.

The sheriff muttered angrily to himself and shook his head, but said nothing more. Dirck guessed that he just liked to make trouble, as all the townspeople said.

Hans's father looked about at the other officials. "It seems the schout has nothing more to say. If you Honorable Lords are agreed?"

They all nodded their heads, "*Ja, ja.*"

"Then," he went on, "I'll ask the clerk to make out a permit for Dirck Jorissen de Webber to sail on the first ship for the fatherland. I will take it myself to General Stuyvesant to sign."

Dirck happily left the courtroom with Hans after the first law case was called. Outside they met Anneke, and the three laughed heartily over the upset schout.

"It serves him right," Anneke giggled, shaking her pale gold braids. "He's a mean Dutchman."

In high spirits, Dirck began to act out his first meeting with Van Ten. He danced as the schout did when he tried to get his plumed hat from Lion. They all laughed so hard at his silliness, they had to drop under the shade of a great tree to find their breath.

"Ho!" said Hans after a moment. "I wonder if one of the real crew of the shipwrecked *Desire* could be the master of Lion?"

Dirck frowned and pulled the dog close to him. "What made you think of that? Didn't someone say that the stranded crew sailed right back to New England after the *Desire* was stolen? On another sloop. Nothing was said about a dog when they made their complaint at Hempstede harbor. *Ach hemel*, I hope . . ."

Anneke gave his yellow hair a playful tug. "Come now, Dirck. Don't be cast down. No one's called for Lion yet, so he's still yours. Don't fret. Oh, do you know what Mother's doing today?" she added cheerfully. "Trimming a samare jacket with the beautiful beaver skin you gave her."

Dirck smiled down at her and tweaked her braid in return. "Girls! So you like the beaver? It's small thanks for all you've done for me. Some day, if I should come back . . ."

Anneke's round cheeks grew pink. "Hans and I both wish you could stay for always. Now everything will be fine if only Father comes home." Tears started in her eyes, and she let a sigh. "And if the

189

English don't attack us. If only peace would come!"

Peace! It did come suddenly to Dirck and Anneke and the people of all New Netherlands. It came with the boom of a cannon from the fort to announce a ship's arrival. It came with the wild ringing of the bells in Saint Nicholas church and the Town Hall.

A large ocean yacht from Amsterdam, Holland, brought the wonderful news on July 18, 1654. But it was not the ship Anneke had waited so long to greet.

The whole town flocked to Town Hall, urged on by Teunis Kraey, the town crier. Dirck stood beside Anneke and her mother as they clutched hands and listened to General Stuyvesant, wearing a coat of mail and long sword.

He began in a booming voice. "Praise ye the Lord. He has secured your gates and blessed your possessions with peace . . ."

When the General had finished, Dirck exclaimed, "Signed between England and the Netherlands last April 15th. Anneke, that was over three months ago, just after I got here! If only there were a faster way to carry news! Now I can sail home for certain," he added happily.

190

He had never heard such cheering and clapping and joy in the streets. The dogs barked, the goats bleated, the geese honked, all adding to the hubbub. Some men even shot off their matchlock guns to celebrate the peace.

Dirck and Anneke ran to dance on the green before the fort with other young people of the town. At dusk bonfires were built there.

It was then, as Dirck stood panting and laughing in the bright glow of the bonfire, that he heard Hans and his father call out to him. Martin Kregier held a paper in his hand. His strong face looked sad.

"The yacht brought mail from the fatherland," he told Dirck. "This letter from your mother came to the city clerk. It asks about you and your uncle Nicholas. There's bad news in it."

Dirck's hand suddenly began to shake, as he took the letter. He could hardly read his mother's writing in the firelight. "Mynheer," she wrote, "we are anxiously awaiting word from Nicholas de Webber and my son, Dirck. We hope that they landed safely in the New Netherlands and no harm has come to them.

"My dear husband Joris died a few days ago. He leaves me alone with two small children besides Dirck. Will you please find my men and ask them to return home at once? I need them both to run our small weaving business."

A pain stabbed Dirck's heart. Father! He threw himself on the grass and his shoulders shook. He would never see Father again! Oh, why had he run away? Poor, dear Mother!

He felt Hans touch his arm. He raised his head, then slowly got to his feet. "Father's dead," he gulped. "It's a terrible shock!" He wiped his face with the back of his sleeve.

Hans clapped an arm around him and said softly, "I understand. I'm very sorry."

Anneke and the others stood around him and tried to comfort him. Dirck straightened his shoulders. "I'm the man of the family now. I have to help take care of Marie and Pieter until they grow up. It means no Latin School or college at Leyden. It means no coming back to New Amsterdam for a long time. Maybe never!" He pressed his lips together firmly.

Anneke looked over at the Kregier Inn. Noises and laughter swirled out of the crowded public room. "Come to our house for the night, Dirck," she suggested. "Mother would like that. She misses my brother so. It's too noisy at Hans's!"

Dirck didn't care now where he slept. "Yes, thanks," he said. "Good night, Hans, Captain

192

Kregier, and everyone. Thank you for your kind words."

He went slowly up the hill from the green with Anneke. She walked silently beside him.

What a fine friend she's been, Dirck thought with a full heart as they passed the old cemetery. He reached over and gently tugged at one of her braids.

"Dirck! Dirck! Wait for me!" Hans was running up the hill, carrying a lantern to light the way.

He stumbled up to them, his lanky hair flying behind his neck. "You'll not guess, ever. The best luck!" he panted. "The pirate Thomas Baxter! He's here, a prisoner!" He could hardly get the words out fast enough.

"Baxter?" Dirck couldn't believe it. "A prisoner here? Tell me!" He shook Hans's arm fiercely.

"A lieutenant just told Father. Baxter was sent here by the Governor of New Haven Plantation. They landed at dusk. The schout couldn't find the jailer at the fort, and you know that jail's mostly for Wilden, anyway. Seems the jailer's out celebrating. So they locked Baxter in the jail room at the Town Hall. Hans Steyn, the deputy, is on guard. There'll be a special hearing tomorrow after the morning sermon."

It seemed too good to be true. "By Saint Nicholas,

I'm glad!" Dirck said. "But why did New Haven send him to us? The people up there wouldn't let our patrol ships into their harbors to capture him."

Hans laughed proudly. "Thanks to my father! Remember when he went on a mission to the New England Governors to complain about Baxter's piracy? That was last April, about the time I went to Fort Orange with you. Father got the Governor of New Haven to promise to send Thomas Baxter here for trial when the war was over. Seems he was as much trouble to them as to us, and they wanted to get rid of him. So the Governor did keep his word."

They talked over this wonderful news sitting on the red velvet chairs in the Van der Grift's cool fore-room. The huge curtained guest bedstead towered over the room in one corner. A square, heavy cupboard stood against a wall on which hung a gold-bordered mirror and several fine etchings.

At nine o'clock it was time for late supper. A breathless Lintie rushed in to spread a linen damask cloth over the table. Anneke's mother had come home, and she took her husband's place in reading a Scripture verse at the table. Both boys stood up and removed their hats while Grace was said.

Dirck could not swallow the bread and milk and

194

the cold meat set before him. He was glad when the meal was over, and they all kissed good night and went off to bed.

He tossed about on the kitchen betse, his thoughts in a whirl. Mixed with his sorrow over his father's death was a great relief over the capture of his enemy, Baxter.

But was he really satisfied? There still were all the questions about the silver half-moon. Where was it now? With Flips, lost, sold, or with the pirate captain?

Somehow, some way, I've got to ask Baxter about it, he decided at last. Even if it does no good.

Then he dozed until the cocks crowed, and the Sunday morning church bells rang. He rose and dressed in his best clothes, the ones Long Mary had made. Carefully, he wiped the dust from his new leather shoes. By the time fat Lintie bustled into the kitchen to stir up the fire and make breakfast, he was ready for church.

He slipped off the boys' bench in the church balcony while the last hymn was loudly sung. He tiptoed down the narrow stairs and pushed open the great wooden doors. Nobody noticed him as he stepped out onto the fort grounds in the blazing sun.

He was on his way to talk to the jailed pirate captain.

In some manner he would talk the guard into letting him speak with Baxter through the barred window of the door. "He just has to let me!" Dirck whispered tensely to Lion, who had been waiting patiently outside.

Dirck hurried out the sally port and skirted the corner of the high sod walls. The dirt lanes of the town were empty. He walked east down to the next lane, Brower, then turned north. He crossed the canal bridge at Hoogh Street and trotted on up that road, which ran past the back entrance to the Town Hall.

The grounds and garden of the Town Hall reached from the river back to Hoogh, which was the next street inland. A square kitchen was tacked on to the rear of the Hall, Dirck thought, trying to remember every detail.

He was halfway up the dusty road when he thought he saw a shadowy figure slip through the back gate and up the path to the Hall's kitchen. Was it really someone? Or was it the movement of sunlight and shadow under the trees? Or the glare of the sun in his eyes?

No, Lion had seen it, too. A low growl sounded

196

in his strong throat, and the fur on his back stood up stiff.

Suddenly Dirck sniffed and looked around. Smoke! Something was afire! He stopped in front of a small cottage with thatched roof, the nearest house to the Town Hall. He saw a plume of smoke rise above it. Then a red tongue of flame shot up from the thatch.

"*Brandt, brandt!* Fire, fire!" he shouted at the top of his lungs. "House afire!"

Lion barked wildly and ran in circles.

Should I run back and tell them at the church, he wondered? Or knock on people's doors?

No, he recalled the leather fire buckets that hung near the Hall's front door, ready for the fire wardens and a bucket line. And the bells! It would be best to ring the bells and send the fire alarm to all the countryside.

Still shouting "Fire!" Dirck ran up to the back gate. He rushed up the garden path to the kitchen door.

"Guard here," he ordered Lion. Then he ran through the empty kitchen and into the long central hall. One glance showed him the two heavy ropes which hung down through a hole in the ceiling from the belfry far above.

Dirck seized them and pulled with all his might.

The jangling, clanging of the bells broke the Sabbath quiet. Surely they must echo across both wide rivers! Three, four, six times he swung on the ropes.

"Stow that!" A man's voice snarled in his ear.

The next thing Dirck knew he was spinning against the wall. As he jumped to his feet Dirck turned his head in time to see a sailor run out the front door. The sailor looked back, a gold earring flashing.

"Flips!" Dirck shouted.

In a flash he knew . . . Flips had set the fire. Flips was here to help Captain Baxter to escape!

_____

CHAPTER FOURTEEN

The Silver Half-Moon

BAXTER *was* escaping! Dirck whirled around just in time to see the pirate run across the hall to the kitchen. The guard had been overcome, the jail room opened. And what a wild look that face with its black eye patch turned on him!

"Stop, you!" Dirck yelled. He didn't care about Flips . . . Baxter was the man to catch.

Dirck rushed after him, but the kitchen door slammed in his face. He shouted a warning to Lion, "After him, boy!"

As he jerked the door open, he heard Lion's deep bark. From the distance, like humming bees, came the shouts of the townsmen.

Then he saw Lion on the back path, blocking Baxter's way and snarling and biting at the pirate's sea boots.

199

Baxter kicked at Lion fiercely and roared, "Take that and that, ye bilge rat."

"Pirates! Help!" Dirck shouted at the top of his voice and dived for Baxter's legs. The man fell with a thud. But he was quick! He leaped to his feet in one bound and started to run down the path.

If the pirate got to the road he might disappear. Perhaps he could find a hiding place with traitors. Dirck realized his chance to find his silver half-moon would be gone. And this wicked man would escape his punishment!

"We can't let him get away," Dirck gasped. He and Lion streaked after Baxter. Just as the pirate reached the gate, the dog leaped.

Baxter stumbled. He fell against the gate and tried to fight off Lion. Dirck jumped on his back, and they went down together.

The pirate struck him again and again, but Dirck stubbornly held on. Would no one ever come?

He shouted desperately, "Help! Over here!"

Then he heard men's footsteps running toward them, surrounding them. Help was here at last!

Someone cried out, "Look! It's a man, a boy, and a dog fighting!"

"It's the pirate," another exclaimed. "Tried to break jail, did he?"

At the same time strong hands separated Dirck from the panting Baxter. He let go Baxter's leg with regret. "Drop, Lion," he ordered as he got unsteadily to his feet. Lion slowly unclamped his jaws from the pirate's arm.

"We caught him . . . Lion and I," Dirck croaked happily. He wiped his hot bruised face with his torn sleeve. His nose was bleeding, but he didn't care. He and Lion together had stopped his enemy, the man who had caused him so much grief and had been responsible for his uncle's death.

Two big Dutchmen jerked the still struggling Baxter to his feet. "It's jail for you again, pirate," they growled.

They pulled his arms behind his back, and when they did so, Dirck saw the gleam of a silver piece under the pirate's torn collar. There, hanging from Baxter's neck on the deerskin cord, was his prized silver half-moon! He had found it again!

With a yelp of joy, Dirck tore the cord from Baxter's neck.

The pirate glared at him from one fierce eye. "Bilge rat! Take care!"

Dirck paid him no heed. "This medal's mine," he told the surprised men. "Thomas Baxter has twice stolen it from me. Now I claim it."

All this while two water bucket lines had formed. They reached from the river, through the Town Hall grounds to the burning house on Hoogh Street. Men, women, and older children passed the full buckets from one to the other and onto the burning cottage. The empty buckets went quickly back the second line to the river for refilling.

The thatched roof was all ablaze. People shouted and ran back and forth. They threw water on the next house, also, to keep the fire from spreading through the neighborhood.

Hans ran up to Dirck with his face streaked with soot. "Father's a fire warden in charge of the fire fighting, and I'm helping," he shouted over the din. "The roof and insides are gone, but the stone walls will stand. The fire won't spread. The owners were at church."

For the first time he noticed Dirck's appearance. "Saint Nicholas! You're a bloody mess! Here's a kerchief." He offered his smudged handkerchief to help stop Dirck's nosebleed.

"Thanks," Dirck said, his face muffled in the cloth. He waved a hand toward the men who were dragging Baxter into the Town Hall. Someone else had gone in search of Schout Van Ten and General Stuyvesant.

202

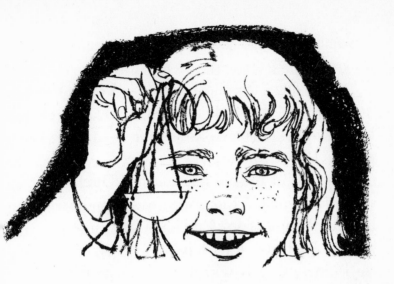

"It's Captain Baxter," he explained as Hans stared. "He tried to escape from the jail room. Lion and I stopped him. Flips, his mate, helped him break out, then got away. Guess Flips started the fire to cover their escape during the excitement of putting the blaze out."

"Saint Nicholas!" Hans gasped, open-mouthed.

"And look, Hans!" With a swoop, Dirck brought the silver half-moon from his breeches pocket. "I found it on Baxter."

"Huzza! You've got it back!" Hans shouted in delight.

Dirck looked at him and laughed, then suddenly they were beating each other on the back and dancing in a circle. After a few dizzy moments Dirck

203

stopped. He knelt and caught the prancing Lion in his arms.

"Good dog," he said proudly. "You're the best dog there is! If it hadn't been for you, we'd never have caught Thomas Baxter. Or found my silver medal. I hope you are always mine."

A twinge of the old fear touched Dirck while he stroked and petted Lion, who was happily wagging his tail. What if Lion's English master came forward, and the dog had to leave him?

"I just can't part with you now," he vowed, and rubbed his face in the thick black fur.

He felt Hans tug at his arm. "Come on, Dirck, let's go tell Father all about this. The bucket lines are breaking up. The fire's out, I suppose."

The sad family who owned the burned house and some of the others were gathering up the fire buckets. They carried them back into their homes and into the Town Hall.

A small group of curious men, women and children began to follow him, Dirck noticed, after the rumors about the cause of the fire began to spread. He was glad his nosebleed had stopped.

Firewarden Martin Kregier, sooty and wet, stood in the muddy lane. He mopped his face and looked over the smoking ruins. His Sunday linen doublet was ruined and his beard looked singed. The boys excitedly told him the story of Baxter's attempted escape.

A look first of amazement then of approval crossed his tanned face. "*Hemel!* Good, good! You did well, Dirck. I'm proud of you and your dog. We will now clap Master Baxter into the fort jailhouse. His mate Flips might have a boat hidden in one of the inlets north of town. We'll search for it at once. We'll find him, too."

He shook Dirck's grubby hand. In front of everyone he said, "New Amsterdam will be grateful to you for what you've done. All loyal citizens were angry with that pirate."

"That's right, Captain," the group crowding around them called out.

Dirck felt his face grow warm with pleasure. "Thank you all. It just happened . . . it was mostly Lion."

All these people, tired and wet, were smiling at him! How friendly they were, so different from that first hateful crowd he met when he landed here! Peace had done this. And perhaps they were sorry for that other time.

"You see," he told them, "I had several old scores to settle with that pirate Baxter. He not only kidnapped me from the *Gilded Beaver* and took away the trade goods my uncle had brought to the New World . . . he also took my family heirloom."

He held up the silver half-moon and then gave it to Hans's father. "There's proof it belongs to my family on the back. See, Captain," Dirck's brown finger pointed out the letters cut into the silver.

Captain Kregier smiled and handed back the medal. "There's no question about it. It's yours, keep it."

A drum rattled, and Dirck heard the court messenger cry out, "The Honorable Director-General of New Netherlands!"

The people stood aside. General Pieter Stuyvesant stumped grandly past them on his silver-banded wooden leg . . . straight up to Dirck and Captain Kregier!

In his hurry to come, the General had forgotten his fine plumed hat. He still wore his black skullcap over his lanky dark hair. Silver buttons crowded down the edge of his long red jacket. A snowy linen and lace "fall" collared his neck, and he carried an ivory cane with gold head.

He tapped Dirck on the shoulder with his cane after Martin Kregier gave him all the news. "*Ach!* Well done, boy . . . er . . . Master de Webber.

Burgomaster Kregier has told me your story before. We are pleased, indeed, with your brave action today. Most unusual, most unusual and highly commendable, my boy!"

"Thank you, Mynheer General," Dirck said. He wished he knew what to do with his hands! "I couldn't have done it without Lion . . . my *pirate* dog," he added wickedly, then shivered at his own daring.

Stuyvesant's steely glance moved over to the dog and back to Dirck. "*Ach*, so! I have signed your sailing permit," he announced. "It will be in Burgomaster Kregier's hands soon. You may sail on the first ship for Holland. Now then," he went on, "as to your late uncle's part of the cargo on the yacht *Gilded Beaver*, which the English pirates captured. It seems that Baxter has sold the cargo in New England, and we can't recover it. The ship can't be found, either."

"I see," Dirck said sadly. All the good things his father had bought and woven, all were gone. Although he had never really hoped to find them again, it would be a great loss to his mother.

"The good Governor of New Haven Plantation seems to think he's done enough by sending the pirate to us. Soon the passengers taken prisoner from the

Gilded Beaver will arrive from Rhode Island. That is the most they will do. You know those English colonies!" The General frowned.

Dirck, Hans, and everyone there nodded wisely. Yes, they knew them, indeed.

Out of the corner of his eye, Dirck caught a glimpse of Schout Van Ten standing behind General Stuyvesant. There was a scowl on his round red face. He looked unhappy at the sight of Dirck talking to Pieter Stuyvesant. I'm not afraid of Van Ten any more, Dirck thought.

He listened to what the General was now saying, unable to believe his ears. "We lately offered a reward of one hundred guilders for every English pirate or privateer caught. Although this Thomas Baxter was handed over to us, you, Dirck de Webber, caught him when he tried to make his escape. I believe you should receive the reward of one hundred guilders for doing this." A smile touched the General's mouth for the first time.

"Thunder and lightning!" The words burst from Dirck and he laughed aloud. "One hundred guilders, Mynheer General?"

It seemed a fortune. Dirck wanted to jump and shout. But instead, he made a bow and thanked the General properly.

"My greatest thanks to you, Mynheer General. It will be an extra help to my widowed mother," he said happily.

"*Hemel!*" Martin Kregier now spoke up, laughing. "Dirck, you speak of your mother and I forgot to ask you. Do you think you could persuade her to come back to New Amsterdam? I can offer her a place as housekeeper at my inn. That means you de Webber children, too."

"Father!" Hans shouted happily.

His father smiled and said, "Maybe your mother will want to sell the de Webber business and would welcome a new home for your family."

Dirck grinned up at the Captain. "Welcome it I will, and I hope she will, too. I'll do my best to persuade her to come, mynheer. With my reward money I can pay all our passage from Rotterdam back to the New World."

"Excellent," declared Pieter Stuyvesant, rubbing his hooked nose. "We need more people here. God be with you, boy." And he limped away to the rattle of the drum.

Hans gave Dirck a bear hug. "By Saint Nicholas, this is more exciting than my trip to the Maquas! You've got to come back, Dirck, and live with me . . . you and Lion and your family."

Would he really be able to get Lion safely on the ship for home, Dirck wondered anxiously? In spite of his good fortune, he had a strange feeling and shivered.

CHAPTER FIFTEEN

Great Day

AFTER DIRCK'S CAPTURE of the pirate, Vrouw Van der Grift insisted that he stay home from the Sunday afternoon sermon and rest.

She and Anneke bathed his bruised face with a herbal water and put one of Long Mary's herb packs on his swollen nose. It cooled and soothed his face in a short while.

Boom! boom! boom! Dirck jumped as the sound broke the Sabbath quiet. "What's that?" he said. "What's happening?"

Anneke squealed, "It's the fort cannon!" She rushed from the kitchen through the foreroom to the front door. The upper part was already open to a fresh sea breeze.

"An ocean ship is coming," she called back to Dirck and her mother. She leaned far out over the closed lower part. She tried to catch a glimpse of a ship on the bay through the trees. "It's at Sandy Point, I suppose, so it will be here in a short while. Let's go meet it."

Dirck knew that when a large ship sailed through the Narrows separating the lower from the upper bay, a signal flag went up on the headland of Sandy Point on Staten Island. From the waterside the flag could be seen to the south across the five-mile stretch of water. Then the soldiers at the fort set off a cannon to announce its approach. This gave the folks from all the countryside time to come to the waterfront to hear the news from Europe or the New World ports.

To Dirck, Vrouw Van der Grift seemed a little flustered as they made ready to meet the ship. She put on her best pearl earrings, and Anneke tied each side of her pale gold hair with pretty ribbons under her lace cap.

"Don't get your hopes up, Anneke," her mother said in a quavery voice. And a moment later she said, "Oh, if the Lord only would send my husband back to us. Surely . . ."

They still haven't given up hope, Dirck thought with pity.

Aloud he said, "Lion and I are coming, too." He

rose from the kitchen betse and slipped on his jerkin, already mended by Anneke's mother. "I've rested long enough. I feel much better." His fingers patted the smooth silver half-moon he hung about his neck. That made up for a lot of things.

They hurried down the hill and stopped for Hans at the Kregier Inn. But he was not at home.

Townsfolk were leaving the church and gathering at the landing place on the hook of land east of the fort. Where was the ship from, was it Dutch or not? Everyone guessed and talked excitedly.

What a thrilling two days, they said. First the peace celebration, then the fire and the pirate's capture. A few noticed Dirck standing with his friends and Lion. They smiled and spoke to him, and this gave him a warm feeling of belonging.

Anneke's mother held a firm grip on her daughter's arm to keep her from dancing about in her excitement. They could see the ship far down the vast bay, coming under a brisk breeze.

Ahead of it ran a small fishing boat with a red sail. Dirck wondered whose it was. It looked familiar to him.

Now the big yacht loomed closer. How beautiful it was with all its white sails blooming above the waves! The western sun caught its high gilded prow

and it gleamed proudly. Above its two high masts a crown of sea gulls circled.

"It just has to be father's ship," Anneke insisted to her mother. "I know it's the *Dolphin*."

Her mother clasped her hands together, afraid to believe. "Wait, child, we don't know yet."

"We can find out!" Dirck said swiftly. "That small boat with the red sails is Kryn's the oysterman's. He's bringing the news."

The little boat had darted in toward the town dock. Everyone pressed forward, straining to catch the oysterman's first words.

Anneke pulled away from her mother with a sharp cry. She clawed her way through the moving crowd and ran out to the dock, her thin-soled cloth slippers skimming over the gravel.

Dirck pushed after her. Behind him, above the hum of the excited people, Hans shouted out, "Ho, Dirck. Wait for me."

They all stopped at the very end of the wharf. They were just ahead of an old gentleman in Puritan dress whom Dirck had never seen before.

Kryn the oysterman looked red and salty as ever to Dirck as he and Hans helped make fast the line. Kryn climbed onto the dock and called out, "She's the *Dolphin*, herself, in port at last!"

215

"Huzza!" Everyone began to shout. They passed the word along, "It's the *Dolphin!*"

"I was at the Narrows when she stopped for a change in the wind," Kryn went on in a loud voice. "Came on ahead to let you all know that skipper and crew are fine. The cargo's safe, in spite of their being thrown off course by a storm and landing in South America. Had a fight with Carribean pirates, too, and won," he told Anneke.

"Oh, happy day!" Anneke laughed and clapped her hands, while tears ran down her pink cheeks. "Father's safely home."

Dirck looked at the grinning Hans. "The cargo's safe!" he exclaimed. "That means we'll have plenty of gunpowder."

"Now our town can protect itself," Hans said happily.

The *Dolphin* sailed slowly past the fort into the East River. Its cannon boomed in a salute. Small figures could be seen moving about the deck and rigging. Soon the yacht would come to anchor in the deep water above the Town Hall. Anneke waved her white cap wildly.

"Heard that the English closed their West Indies ports to Dutch traders. So your father had trouble finding powder . . ." Kryn stopped talking and looked over Dirck's shoulder at the old gentleman in Puritan clothes.

"By a whale's flippers," he said heartily, "if it isn't my Massachusetts trader friend, Mynheer Isaac Allerton!"

Kryn pushed past Dirck and his friends. He clasped the elderly trader by the hand. "I've not seen you since the loss of the *Desire*," he boomed. "At first I didn't know it was your sloop."

"Aye, 'twas a new one," the merchant said in Dutch. "I just came to town from Boston. I couldn't get back here while the colony was preparing for war. They tell me that it was Thomas Baxter who stole and wrecked the *Desire*. It's a total loss."

Isaac Allerton was the English owner of the *Desire*, the sloop he'd been wrecked on? Dirck gulped. Then a thought struck him and he feared his heart would stop.

"Everything lost? Not so, not so," Kryn declared. He grasped Dirck's unwilling shoulder and turned him to face the owner of the sunk ship . . . and the owner of Lion?

The merchant trader looked at Dirck, his long chin pressed against his lace-edged collar. His eyes seemed kind in his seamed face. "Good day, lad."

Dirck mumbled something.

217

"This here is the lad I found on the shore near Eaton's Neck," Kryn said. "Baxter took him from the *Gilded Beaver* and put him aboard your sloop after the pirates stole it at Hempstede. The black dog aboard brought him to shore during the storm, he thinks. Could the dog be yours?"

Isaac Allerton nodded. "I've learned your story, Dirck, a half-hour ago from the good Captain Kregier. And truly sorry I am about your troubles. Yes, the Newfoundland dog is mine. He had been given to me by a friend, and he's almost a year old. He liked ships, so my skipper took him on the trip to Long Island. Baxter stole the *Desire* while it was anchored in harbor and Lion was aboard alone." The merchant held out his hand to Lion. He spoke in English, "Come, Blackie."

Lion, who had been sitting on Dirck's feet, rose up at the English words. He wagged his tail and licked Mr. Allerton's hand when the merchant patted him.

"He remembers me." The merchant was pleased. "I saw him there, and thought he was the one."

"I've looked after him the best I could, mynheer," Dirck said miserably. "He's the best dog in the whole world. He thinks his name is Lion, now."

First he'd lost his father, and now it was Lion. Dirck thought his heart would break. But Lion

218

didn't belong to him any more. He straightened his shoulders and lifted his chin.

"I . . . I know you'll want to take him away with . . . with . . . you," he managed to croak.

Mr. Allerton put his hand on Dirck's shoulder. "I think Lion would not want to give you up, my boy. I had him only a short time. He's more yours than mine. Captain Kregier says the dog has helped you grow up. You've earned the right to be his master."

"You mean he's all mine? Oh, thank you, thank you, sir!" Like magic, his sorrow changed to joy. He wrung Mr. Allerton's hand in gratitude.

Then he turned to Anneke and Hans, a wide grin on his face. "Did you hear? Lion's mine, all mine!"

Anneke had listened to their talk with one ear while she watched a scow move out to the *Dolphin*. She began to hop up and down. Dirck could see that she was beside herself with excitement.

"Yes, Dirck, isn't it wonderful? I was praying that he might give you Lion. But look, they're loading the scow." She pointed out to the *Dolphin*. "That's Father climbing down into it, I know. Oh, hurry!" she called over the babble of the crowd.

Dirck laughed from sheer happiness. What a great day this turned out to be. Anneke's father safely returned, the pirate Baxter captured, Lion really his

own dog now! and the silver half-moon once again
his. There was even a place for him and his family
in this New World, which was no longer strange.
In his heart he knew that Father and Uncle Nick
would approve.

He felt Lion's cold nose in his hand. Looking
down, he saw that the dog wanted to show off his
latest trick. There on the edge of the dock he was
sitting up and begging!

Dirck laughed again. He slipped Lion a bit of
cruller from his pocket. Then he knelt down and
hugged the big black dog close.

"Good old pirate Lion," he said. "You're my dog
now. Forever and ever!"

NOTES ON THE CHARACTERS IN
PIRATE DOG

These people in the story really lived in New Amsterdam (New York) in 1654:

Thomas Baxter, called "pirate" by the Dutch, lived for years in New Amsterdam. In 1653 he went over to the English and claimed to have privateer papers from the Plantation (colony) of Rhode Island to "goe against the Dutch." He caused trouble in the Connecticut colonies as well as with his piracy against the Dutch, and was sent to New Amsterdam by the English. Eventually he escaped from jail and returned to New England.

Martin Kregier was a leading citizen and burgomaster (city official), popular innkeeper, captain of militia, trader and fire warden.

Cornelis Van Tienhoven ("Van Ten") was schout-fiscal, or sheriff-mayor, of New Amsterdam. He was a friend of General Pieter Stuyvesant, and had a reputation for being quarrelsome and dishonest.

Pieter Stuyvesant was a soldier and Director-General of the Dutch colony of New Netherlands for the West India Company. He was not called "Governor." Despotic and intolerant, he did not hold the love of the people.

Jan Baptiste Van Rensselaer, one of the sons of the founder of the vast colony of Rensselaerswyck on the site of Albany, New York, spent a number of years in America directing the business of the colony. He was at odds with Pieter Stuyvesant over ownership of some land and over political control.

Sam Louw, ("*Low*") was a rascal who worked with and helped Thomas Baxter and his gang. They met at night in his house. As punishment for his dishonesty and treason, General Stuyvesant banished him and confiscated his house.

Isaac Allerton, a New England trader who landed with the pilgrims on the Mayflower, grew wealthy trading with the Dutch. He lived parttime in New Amsterdam in a stone house on a hill behind his river warehouse and dock, outside the city wall.

Paulus Van der Grift, a leading citizen, alderman, and merchant-trader with a warehouse, was also a ship's captain, and an officer of the West India Company. He lived in a fine house on "de Heere Straet" near the wall.

Other persons mentioned:

Dr. Hans Kierstede, best known of the town's few Doctors.

Teunis Kraey, the town crier.

Governor Eaton of New Haven Plantation, who

222

returned Thomas Baxter to Pieter Stuyvesant for trial.

Arent Jansen, deputy and later jailer at the Stadt Huis, the Town Hall.

Gabriel Carpesy, town herdsman.

Great Arrow, Cayenquirago, a Maquas (Mohawk) sachem.

Arent Van Hattem, city official, one of two burgo-masters.

Adrien Van der Donck, lawyer and enemy of Pieter Stuyvesant. He published *A Description of New Netherlands* about 1650 in a protest against General Stuyvesant to the Dutch government in Amsterdam, Holland.